MORNING OF A SABRE

MORNING OF A SABRE

Catherine Darby

Chivers Press • Thorndike Press
Bath, England   Waterville, Maine USA

This Large Print edition is published by Chivers Press, England, and by Thorndike Press, USA.

Published in 2001 in the U.K. by arrangement with the author.

Published in 2001 in the U.S. by arrangement with Robert Hale Limited.

U.K. Hardcover   ISBN 0–7540–4511–0   (Chivers Large Print)
U.K. Softcover   ISBN 0–7540–4512–9   (Camden Large Print)
U.S. Softcover   ISBN 0–7862–3327–3   (General Series Edition)

The text of this Large Print edition is unabridged.
Other aspects of the book may vary from the original edition.

Set in 16 pt. New Times Roman.

Printed in Great Britain on acid-free paper.

British Library Cataloguing in Publication Data available

Library of Congress Cataloging-in-Publication Data

Darby, Catherine.
    Morning of a sabre / by Catherine Darby.
        p.   cm.
    ISBN 0–7862–3327–3 (lg. print : sc : alk. paper)
    1. Large type books. I. Title.
PR6052.L335 M67 2001
823'.914—dc21   2001027236

CHAPTER ONE

It was agreed in the neighbourhood that Mrs Fanny Sabre Webber was an exceedingly handsome woman. Though she was close on sixty her skin was still remarkably clear, her blue eyes almost as large as when she had been a girl, her red-gold hair faded to a pale silvery grey. She wore the smartest fashions though it was some years since she had returned as a widow from the United States, accompanied by her three daughters. The eldest, Pearl, had married her cousin, Larch, and perished in the train crash that killed them both. The second, Garnet, had eloped with an actor and lived estranged in London. Only the youngest, Rose, was still at Sabre Hall and likely to remain there, for it was unlikely that anyone would want to marry a girl whose legs were of unequal length.

'Not that you don't have a pretty face and a sweet nature,' Fanny had told her, 'but that thick-soled shoe is so ugly, my love. You will be fortunate if a gentleman offers for you out of anything more than pity.'

Mother was probably right. She usually was, though that didn't make the situation any easier. There were times when Rose would have given her dark blue eyes that slanted upward between thick lashes and her dark

1

shining hair for two legs that were the same length. There were times when she sat by the window in her bedroom, looked out over the moor, and dreamed of how it might be if a man sat by her, his arm around her waist. She had not yet known such a thing and her fear was that she would never know about it. She would become like her mother's twin sister, Esther, who after a brief marriage had returned to Sabre Hall and now was almost faded into its walls so much a part of it had she become. Yet even Aunt Esther had known the embrace of a man and borne a son.

That same son who had inherited Sabre Hall when Grandmother Fausty had died was walking across the garden towards her. She watched him from beneath her lashes, the wild rose colour coming and going in her cheeks. Sabre Ashton, in his late thirties, was twenty years her senior but that, in Rose's eyes, only added to his attraction for her. His dark red hair waved over his shapely head and his grey eyes and clean-cut features echoed the lineaments of his grandfather's portrait which hung in the dining room.

He had paused by the bench on which she sat and was looking down at her.

'If you are going to ask me if I've nothing better to do with my time than idle it away, you may save your breath,' she said tartly.

'My name isn't Fanny,' he retorted equably, sitting beside her. 'You may act the lotus for

2

ever if you choose—and a very charming lotus you make too.'

He often said things like that. They meant nothing, she told herself. Sabre was an attractive man who, though he had avoided any entanglement of marriage, liked women as much as they liked him.

'Cousin Sabre.' She spoke abruptly, her small hands clenching. 'Do you ever think that we are a very strange family?'

'In what way?' He had cocked an eyebrow but his glance was keen.

'Well.' She hesitated, biting the full lower lip that gave a sense of sensuality to her small face. 'Well, Grandmother Fausty came from Ireland to marry Grandfather Earl and he died and left her with two sets of twins.'

'That's unusual certainly,' he agreed, 'but scarcely strange.'

'Then Uncle Patrick was killed, leaving an illegitimate son,' Rose said, 'and Aunt Esther eloped with Philip Ashton and never told any of us that she'd had a child, and Aunt Gobnait ran off with Mother's first husband and lived with him at Batley Tor.'

'And I was reared in ignorance of all this,' he completed.

'Perhaps Aunt Esther didn't wish you to know that one day you would inherit the house and the mill,' Rose ventured. 'Perhaps she wanted you to make your own way in the world.'

'A pleasantly romantic idea,' he said, his glance amused. 'The barefoot boy becomes lord of the manor! Not that I know much about the woollen industry. Aunt Fanny has been the most tremendous help in that direction.'

'Mother,' said Rose, solemnly quoting, 'is a marvel.'

'And so are you.' There was warmth in his face when he looked at her. 'Leaving America and coming to a strange country can't have been easy and so much has happened since.'

'That's true.' She was silent for a few moments, remembering.

When the man who had been Fanny's husband and Gobnait's lover had died, the sisters had married. Gobnait had wed a former suitor and lived with him in Africa until his death and Fanny had sailed to America, married an elderly sea-captain, and reared her three daughters until her husband's death when she had returned with them to Yorkshire. Pearl, the eldest, had married her bastard cousin, Larch, and Garnet had run off with a rakish young actor. Then Grandmother Fausty had died and the son of Aunt Esther's brief, almost forgotten marriage had returned to claim the property.

'You've had no word from your sister?' he enquired.

'Nothing. Perhaps she's married by now. I wish you knew her. She's so full of life.'

There was a wistful note in her voice that roused his sympathy. This lonely house where the two widowed sisters lived was no place for a lively young girl. The other sister, Gobnait, occupied the small stud farm over at Batley Tor where she had lived for years, openly defying convention, with her sister's husband. There had been, he considered, too many deaths, too many secrets in the Sabre family.

'You're full of life yourself,' he countered. 'It ought not to be wasted in a place like this.'

'Oh, I never wanted to go into society,' she assured him. 'Mother promised Pearl that she could have a season in London, but she married Larch and Garnet ran off to London anyway. I don't think I'd exactly shine in the polite world even if I wanted to!'

'Don't underestimate yourself. You're a lovely girl.'

'With a gimpy leg.' She spoke without self-pity. 'Anyway I love Sabre Hall. It's the most beautiful house I ever saw, much grander than the house we had in New York.'

She glanced towards it as she spoke, affection in her expression. It was not, to an objective eye, a beautiful house at all. Of stark grey stone, with every sprig of ivy ruthlessly trimmed away, it stood foursquare, looking down over the valley where the river ran past the long weaving shed and smoke-blackened chimney of the Sabre mill. The garden at the side bore the stamp of Fanny's personality. Its paths were straight, its box hedges trimmed, its beds free from weeds or couch-grass. There had been a time when roses had been grown there but, on her return from the States, Fanny had rooted them up, declaring the petals fell too soon and made the ground messy. From childhood Fanny had never been able to endure a mess.

'It's a grand house certainly,' he agreed, the lilt in his accent a legacy of his Irish upbringing. 'More suited to a big family than a bachelor.'

'Perhaps you won't always be a bachelor,' Rose said.

'Well, I've yet to find the woman I could bear to spend the rest of my life with,' he grinned.

She bit her lip and looked down at her hands, wishing that she could find the courage to ask him about the women with whom he did spend time. It was, after all, none of her business

'And what about you?' He smiled at her. 'Have you seen any local gentleman you fancy?'

Wanting to say 'you', she shook her dark head.

'Well, you're young enough.' He spoke with a casual affection that hurt her. 'You should take your time choosing.'

'Or Mother.' She made a comical little grimace.

'Your mother,' Sabre agreed, 'is a formidable lady. Also one in whom there is clearly much to be admired.'

'She's had a hard life,' Rose said solemnly. 'It can't be easy to marry a man and then have him run away to live with one's sister.'

'And bear his child,' he reminded her.

'Cousin Abigail,' she nodded. 'She and Cousin Larch were married when Mother brought us here from New York and then Abigail died and Pearl married Larch.'

'Tell me about your sisters,' he invited.

'Oh, but I've talked of them before,' she protested smilingly. 'Pearl was lovely. Mother always says that she was like herself when young. Pearl was always very much the young lady.'

'And Garnet is the one who rides.'

'Nearly as well as you do,' she assured him. 'She is like Aunt Gobnait in feature, though younger of course. Mother will not have her name mentioned since she ran off with that actor.'

'It was a rebellious act certainly.'

'And against Mother rebellion has to be revolution before it can hope to succeed.' Conscious of her disloyalty she giggled nervously.

'And you have no desire to rebel?'

'Not more than once a day,' Rose said, blushing as he laughed. Sabre always made her feel witty and amusing, but she guessed he was the kind of man who made most women feel like that. Even her mother lost her diamond hardness and became velvet when Sabre spoke to her in a certain way.

'Isn't there anything you want to do?' His tone was serious again. She had the comforting sensation that he was genuinely interested and would help her if he could.

'Sometimes,' she said, hesitating, 'I wish that Grandmother Fausty had lived long enough for her to visit Ireland with me. She was always talking about returning to her childhood home, you know. She thought it would be as it had been when she was a girl.'

'The Famine altered a lot, I'm told,' Sabre said.

'Of course you know Ireland well!' she exclaimed. 'Tell me of it, Sabre. Was it as Grandmother Fausty said with the mist rising over the mountains and the pigs fat in their sties?'

'Some of it is still like that,' he said. 'There's still the mist though the pigs are leaner now. I spent time there as a boy and I loved the long summers more than any season in Italy.'

'And you'll know all the Sullivans, all the Irish relatives,' she said. 'Mother never talks about them.'

'I reckon Aunt Fanny prefers to remember the Sabres,' he said. 'No Sullivan ever made a fortune in India, then came into Yorkshire to build a house and a mill. Only Grandmother

8

ever broke away from Ireland.'

'And Mother would say the best thing she ever did was to marry into the Sabre family,' Rose said, smiling.

'Well, there's nothing to be ashamed about in the Sullivan strain,' he told her. 'They may not have position or money but they took good care of me when I was a lad.'

'I suppose most of Grandmother's brothers and sisters are dead now,' Rose said.

Like an echo in her mind were Fausty's words.

'I was the eldest of eight. Bridie, God rest her soul, married late and I never met her two children. I'm told they're dead too. Cathy and Danny and Peg are gone. They didn't make old bones at all.'

'Aunt Mary is in the Convent of Our Lady Immaculate,' Sabre was saying. 'She's the Prioress there and a very saintly soul.'

'Oh,' Rose said flatly.

'Which doesn't mean she's dull,' he said, smiling at her expression. 'She's a very lively, sharped-tongued old lady, I promise you. And the uncles, Sean and Stevie, are as graceless a pair of elderly rascals as ever whistled an Irish jig.'

'Oh, but I would like to meet them!' she cried.

'Well, I may take a trip there myself when time permits,' he said easily. 'Right now I'm enjoying being the lord of the manor too much to go travelling again.'

'And I have never travelled at all save once across the Atlantic,' Rose said.

'Which is further than most people go.'

'But in New York we lived in an ordinary brownstone house,' she said earnestly, 'and we never went anywhere. Father was a retired sea-captain and his health wasn't good, so we lived very quietly until his death and then Mother decided to come back to England.'

She fell silent for a space, remembering herself as a limping twelve-year-old seeing the frowning bulk of Sabre Hall for the first time. She had loved the bright-eyed old lady born in the first year of the century whose grandchildren, legitimate and bastard, lived at Sabre Hall, and she had loved her cousin Larch, result of an affair between her Uncle Patrick and an Irish cousin. Larch had been married at that time to Cousin Abigail whose very existence must have been an affront to Fanny. Abigail had been the child born of the affair between Fanny's husband and sister and her presence must have been a constant reminder of their treachery. Abigail had been a sweet, plain girl whose tragic death had plunged Larch into a depression from which Pearl had only partly rescued him.

'Cheer up or Aunt Fanny will think I've been bullying you,' Sabre said, nodding in the direction of the house.

Fanny was emerging from a side door, her

10

step brisk, her head high. The two watching her as she walked towards them were struck by the same thought. For all the varied events that had shaped her life and character she was never less than pristine fresh. This morning she wore a high necked dress of black silk with deep pink ribbons threaded through the yoke, and matching ribbons trimmed the tiny black cap perched on her smoothly coiffured head. Though she was near sixty there were few lines on her face and her cornflower blue eyes were sharp as they rested on her daughter and her nephew.

She spoke tranquilly enough, her pretty mouth curving into a smile.

'So there you are! I was going down to the mill but, since you're here, perhaps you'd like to ride down there yourself. There are some orders that came a few days since which need to be sorted out.'

'I'll go.' Sabre rose, stretching.

'If you have nothing to do,' Fanny said, her blue eyes switching to Rose, 'why don't you go with him? Esther has made some toffee for the children.'

She made a slight face, drawing them into the little joke against her twin. Esther had the kindest heart in the world and was the most unreliable cook in Yorkshire.

'I'll take it,' Rose said, 'unless Sabre's busy.'

'Sabre will enjoy your company,' Fanny said.

'I always do,' Sabre said, smiling down at his

11

cousin. 'You're not dressed for riding so I'll harness the trap.'

'You need your bonnet, my love.' Fanny gave Rose a little push and took her place on the garden seat. 'Put on the straw one. It looks cooler than the blue.'

'The straw's for best,' Rose objected.

'And best clothes should not only be worn on high days and holidays,' Fanny said playfully. 'A charming bonnet distracts the attention from your leg. Hurry now. Keeping a gentleman waiting is a pastime to be indulged in only when one has caught the gentleman in question.'

'Mother!' Rose looked in agony after her cousin's tall, retreating figure.

'Hurry now, dear.' Fanny gave an approving nod as Rose went obediently away.

It was a fine, warm morning with just the right chill on the breeze that Fanny liked. She averted her gaze from her daughter's limping gait and looked instead at the neatly weeded flower beds. The garden was confined by the low stone wall beyond which the green lawn stretched to the edge of the moor. The sight of that wall, holding back the untamed loveliness of the landscape, gave her a feeling of security. She had always preferred people and places she could control.

After a few moments, for she seldom sat still for longer, she rose and re-entered the house, taking the path that led round to the front door. It being summer the door was ajar and she passed through into the wide entrance hall. A graceful staircase led up to a long gallery, patterned with lozenges of brilliant colour from the square panels of stained glass in the wall behind. On the left between two doors a narrow flight of steps gave access to the two rooms that Sabre now used as bedchamber and dressing room. These rooms were the same ones in which she had spent her brief married life with Matthew Lawley. She compressed her lips firmly together against past pain, glanced in at the drawing room and then, pushing the door wider, entered the dining room.

This had always been her favourite room. It had been kept very much as it had been when Sabre Hall had first been built in the eighteenth century, crimson curtains and carved furniture against dark panelled walls. Over the fireplace hung the portrait of her father, Earl Sabre. He had died before she was born and so imagination had to take the place of memory. He had been handsome and charming. His likeness showed waving auburn hair and a lazy smile. He had been brave and he had been wealthy. All her life Fanny had hoped to find a man who would match the idea she had of her dead father. Her brother, Patrick, and Patrick's bastard son, Larch, had resembled him in looks but both had been lazy, tolerant men with nothing in them of the steel she possessed herself. Now Sabre Ashton, Esther's son, was the master of Sabre Hall. When he stood near the portrait, the resemblance was startling.

She was still not certain how she felt about her nephew. Esther, gentlest and dreamiest of the three Sabre girls, had committed the one reckless act of her life when she had eloped with Philip Ashton. Within a couple of years he had died of a fever in Italy and she had came back to Sabre Hall, giving no hint of the fact that she had borne the child who would eventually inherit the property. There was a slyness in Esther that was hard to penetrate. A slight frown creased Fanny's smooth brow and, for an instant as she glanced at the portrait, her expression bore something other than hero-worship, her lips moving silently.

'What possessed you to will the property as you did, Father? To have it pass to the next legitimate male heir and, if there were none, down through the female line was bound to cause conflict.'

No doubt Earl Sabre had expected his infant son, Patrick, to survive to become master but Patrick, for all his lazy good-humour, would have been most unsuitable. His early and violent death, before he could marry his ramshackle, Irish cousin, had removed both him and his bastard Larch from the succession. Fanny's lips curved again into their customary smile. While her mother had lived

14

she had held the property in trust and, on her death, it would have passed to Gobnait and then, as Gobnait had no legitimate issue, to Fanny and her three daughters. Everything had been so neat, but then Mother had died and Esther had released her bombshell. The boy she and Philip Ashton had produced had arrived to claim his inheritance and, to every question as to why she had kept his existence a secret, Esther had only replied vaguely that she had thought it better so. It was almost, Fanny thought, as if she didn't trust her.

She turned from the picture and went to the hall again. The door at the far side opened into the study, a room that Rose had made peculiarly her own. Here the girl sat, hour after hour, reading her way through volumes of books that lined the walls. The archway beyond gave access to the inner hall and the big kitchen.

Fanny started up the stairs, her step quiet and brisk. All her gestures were neat and economical, each one rounded and complete, unlike her sisters'. Gobnait strode everywhere, kicking aside her hampering skirts, and Esther floated, her hands making vague gestures in the air.

The sunlight made dazzling patterns in the air and her face was dyed with colour as she went along the gallery to the long corridor with two bedchambers at each side and the staircase at the end which led down to the kitchen. The first of the bedrooms was occupied by Maggie, who boasted the title of housekeeper, but was actually general maid of all work, and next to her was Rose's room. Fanny opened the door and went in. From the window she looked out over the garden and the lawn to where the pony-trap was bowling down the track. They would be out of the way for at least two hours.

The room had originally been occupied by Esther when she was a girl. From this room she had slipped out to marry Philip Ashton and returned to it as a widow. Now Esther slept in Fausty's old room, her gentle personality making no impression on the atmosphere of lively enthusiasm left by Fausty. Rose had Esther's old room to herself. Nothing had altered since Garnet had left and Pearl had died with Larch in the train crash, but Rose was no Esther. Evidence of her own personality was scattered throughout the room. The book she had been reading lay open on the bedside table and her red dressing gown was flung over the back of a chair. Rose was not the tidiest of girls.

Her mother moved to the dressing table and slid open the top drawer. Under the pile of gloves and handkerchiefs was the Diary bound in red morocco in which Rose made infrequent entries. She opened it, flipped through the earlier pages, and came to the latest entry in Rose's spiky hand.

'S. stayed in York overnight. Buying a new saddle. He told me I looked good on a horse, but it was said casually. Still one must note compliments especially when they are rare!'

There was nothing else. Little that was exciting ever happened to Rose, but the entries, almost without exception, mentioned S. Fanny closed the book and put it back in its concealing place. Only Rose, she thought, would be so naive as to imagine her girlish outpourings would remain secret. It was clear to the least discerning eye that she was half in love with her cousin already. Of Sabre's feelings Fanny was not so certain. He was a virile, attractive man whose nights away from home were not, she guessed, spent in the company of his male friends. Time would tell, but she sometimes had the feeling that the weeks and months were flying faster. Sabre might very well meet someone else whom he envisaged as mistress of Sabre Hall. Rose had to be that person. Fanny's narrow hands clenched as if she vowed on the hilt of a sword and she went quietly out.

Esther would be taking a nap. Fanny hesitated, decided against waking her, and crossed the passage to her own room. It was, as always, neat enough for official inspection, the green bedspread smoothed flat, the hangings tied back with yellow ribbon, the mirrors polished to a shining brilliance that reflected the yellow blossoms printed on the curtains and the shelf on which her collection of wooden dolls sat. She cast an approving glance at them. Dolls, unlike people, never disappointed one, never became untidy, never argued or rebelled. There swam into her mind a picture of her second daughter, Garnet. Garnet was too much like Gobnait for Fanny ever to love her without reservation, but she had done her best for the girl. And Garnet had betrayed her by running off with a rapscallion actor whom Fanny had already paid off. It was hard to believe that Garnet could have had so little pride. She shook her head to banish the tormenting image, allowed her thoughts to dwell briefly on Pearl who had remained perfect and obedient by dying, and resumed her thoughts of Rose and Sabre.

The girl was certainly very pretty with a lively intelligence and a sharp sense of humour. Fanny had little humour herself but she could appreciate it in others. It was a thousand pities that she was lame. On the other hand Sabre had a kindly heart and pity might easily be mistaken for love. There were worse reasons for marriage. With Rose as Sabre's wife her own control of the household and of the mill would remain unchallenged.

'I thought I heard you in here.' Esther's voice followed a tap on the door.

'And I thought I was moving quietly. Did I wake you?'

'I was having a little think,' Esther said,

never willing to admit that she'd been asleep.

'Rose went down to the mill with Sabre. She took the toffee.'

'It didn't set very well,' Esther confessed. 'It was a bit lumpy.'

'Well, I don't expect the children will mind.' Fanny gave her a kindly look, wishing that Esther would, for once, neaten herself. Her long, silver-white hair was already escaping from its pins and the ends of her shawl were bedraggled. She was drifting over to the window now, fingering the silk of the curtains.

'Rose went with Sabre,' she repeated in a thoughtful tone. 'They seem very fond of each other, don't they? I've been wondering if it might not lead to something more. If your daughter and my son were to—well, to marry, that would be pleasant, don't you think?'

'Marriage?' Fanny let the word hang in the air for a moment. 'I never thought of it myself, Esther, but you may be right.'

CHAPTER TWO

'How do I look?'

Garnet might as well have addressed the question to the air, so complete was the indifference with which it was received. Nicholas Brocklehurst lay on his back, arms crossed behind his head, eyes half-closed,

19

though she knew very well that he was not asleep. He had a habit that infuriated her of withdrawing to a far place even when they were in the same room.

Shrugging, she turned again to the mirror, tweaking the veil of her hat with shapely, nervous fingers. The little toque of cream spotted net was decorated with two small satin bows of the same brown as the stripes on her cream dress. Her heavy hair was wound into a chignon at the back of her head and the long lids of her grey eyes were brushed with green shadow. At nineteen she was not beautiful but life in the city had given her a veneer of sophistication that made men turn to take a second look.

For her own part she seldom noticed them. For two years Nicholas Brocklehurst had filled her heart and mind, and no other man had entered upon the horizon. There were moments however when she felt a tired disgust at her own weakness. Nicholas was handsome and could be charming when he took the trouble, but she could not avoid remembering that he had once accepted the bribe her mother had offered and left the district. That he had welcomed her when she followed him and that much of the money had been spent on her wardrobe could not obliterate the nagging doubts that sometimes entered her mind.

'Where are you going anyway?' Nicholas

enquired, opening his eyes.

'Out to supper.' She waited for his reaction and, when none came, demanded impatiently, 'Don't you want to know where?'

'Darling, there's nothing worse than a suspicious man,' he yawned. 'I assume that you're going for a respectable supper-party with a group of lady friends.'

'I don't know any ladies,' Garnet said flatly.

'Poor love! Do you miss being respectable?' he teased. 'We theatrical folk have always been regarded as rogues and vagabonds.'

'We theatrical folk,' she said tartly, 'have been out of work for the past couple of months, or had you forgotten that?'

'I'm not likely to. You remind me of it at least a dozen times a day.'

'And the rent needs to be paid!'

'Which is why you just bought a new dress and hat? Not that they aren't charming, but you will look a little foolish walking the streets in them when you are thrown out of this lodging!'

'You'll be walking the streets yourself,' she pointed out.

'Not me, darling.' He gave her his lazy smile. 'I think that I'll always find somewhere to lay my head.'

'In a lady's lap no doubt.'

'In your lap, if that's possible.' He half-rose, stretching out his hand, but she evaded it, displeasure still in her voice.

21

'Well, you stay and contemplate the future, while I go to my supper. I'll be home before eleven.'

'I'm not going anywhere.' He leaned back again.

Garnet, frowning at him, noticed the dark shadow on his jawline, the greasiness of the lock of hair that flopped over his brow. His habits were becoming increasingly slovenly and it hurt her heart to see his deterioration.

'Do try to tidy yourself up before I get back,' she began.

'Why, are you bringing the Prince of Wales home?' he enquired.

'Don't think I couldn't. Not that I would, to a room like this.'

She looked round the littered apartment with distaste.

'Darling, you sound like a wife,' he complained.

'And I'm not likely to become that, am I?' she said sweetly.

'When I've made my name as the finest Shakespearean actor of this generation I'll walk you up the aisle,' he said.

'By that time,' Garnet said, losing patience, 'you'll have to get someone to wheel us both in a bathchair!'

'I'll find work. Don't I always?'

'Well, I'm not holding my breath,' she said stonily, taking up her gloves and parasol, and moving to the door. When she heard his chuckle she didn't trouble to look back.

At the foot of the staircase she paused, dreading to hear the landlady's enquiring tone, but the dingy hallway was empty. She opened the door and went out into the early evening, raising her face to the narrow strip of sky. In London, even in summer, acrid yellow fog drifted around the chimney pots and stung the eyes and nostrils. She had a brief and sudden longing for the wide, clear skies that roofed the moors about Sabre Hall. Then she went, head elegantly high, down the street, ignoring the catcalls of a few urchins who were swinging on the railings. She would have liked to take a cab but cabs cost money and she had none to spare. Fortunately she had only a reasonable distance to walk, and she did so briskly, glad when she had left the somewhat unsalubrious district in which the lodgings were situated and came out into a more genteel neighbourhood. A few nannies were walking their charges home and a red-coated soldier chatted at one corner to a girl in a flowered bonnet. Garnet glanced at them with unconscious wistfulness as she crossed the road and made her own way down to the small theatre where the auditions were being held.

Thank the Lord that Nicholas had not enquired closely as to her destination. This was the first time she had asserted her independence and set out to find a job by herself. A small theatre group was being formed with the intention of reviving the classics and a young woman was required to play second leads. She had heard of the opportunity through the grapevine along which gossip of parts being cast filtered, and said nothing to Nicholas. It was not that he would have objected to her working, but he might have insisted on going with her to the audition, forcing himself on the notice of the management, making her nervous by too audible encouragement. In one way he was proud of her. In another way he took a subtle pleasure in diminishing her. Side by side with the physical infatuation she still felt for him was growing the desire to be herself alone, to show him that she had an identity apart.

She went in through the stage door, gave her name to the doorkeeper, and was motioned to a chair in the wings. On stage a girl with yellow hair aureoled by the flaring gaslight was tearing Ophelia to shreds. She was pretty but her voice was too squeaky and Garnet sensed discontent in the darkened auditorium beyond.

The girl came off, wearing the nervously defiant smile of one who knows she could have done better. Garnet gave her an answering smile which she hoped was not too sympathetic and, hearing her name called, walked out onto the bare stage. As usual the glare of the lights hit her and she blinked, wishing it were possible to see clearly into the darkness beyond the footlights.

'Miss Webber, have you your piece prepared?'

The voice was a gentleman's voice. Now she could dimly discern half a dozen figures scattered about.

'Yes, sir. I intend to do Lady Macbeth.'

'The sleepwalking scene, I suppose?' There was a hint of resignation in the voice.

'No, sir. The letter scene.'

'Very well. Begin when you're ready.'

But she never would be ready, Garnet thought with bleak self-knowledge. She was not really an actress at all. Sleeping with an actor and playing the occasional small part was no proof of talent. Not for the first time she experienced a wave of furious anger against her mother. Had it not been for Fanny's interference her passion for Nicholas Brocklehurst might well have died a natural death.

'Miss Webber?' The voice was faintly impatient.

Oh, but she could imagine Fanny plotting the murder of Duncan, turning a laudable ambition into a savage intrigue, rooting it in domesticity. She could see Fanny with her curving smile and hear the sweetly precise tones as she mused aloud 'The raven himself is hoarse that croaks the fatal entrance of Duncan under my battlements'. She could hear her own voice, husky but clear; was aware of the little stabbing movements her hands made with the parasol. Her voice died into silence and beyond the footlights someone coughed.

'Can you undertake a comic piece?' the voice that had spoken before asked.

'Mrs Malaprop?' she ventured.

'If you must.' The tone was resigned again.

Garnet took a deep breath and launched into it, conscious that she was sinking before she had fairly begun. She was too tall, too gauche, too much aware of the farcical elements in the character to play it with the lofty ignorance the role demanded. She ended on a dying fall and stood, waiting for dismissal.

'Miss Webber, would you be good enough to join us down here?' someone asked.

She descended the steps at the side of the apron stage and went, vision improving, past the small orchestra pit to where three or four gentlemen were seated in the stalls. Two of them, with their opera capes and open cravats, were clearly managers. A third was a tall, distinguished looking elderly man with silver hair brushed back from a high forehead.

'Miss Webber.' It was one of the managers who addressed her. 'Allow me to introduce myself. Septimus Ryan, and this is my brother, Wendell. We are planning this new venture as a joint undertaking.'

'Sir.' She shook hands, trembling a little now that the ordeal of the audition was behind her.

'What experience have you had?' the one called Wendell was enquiring.

'Not very much. I played small character roles in a fit up company and I had one London season,' Garnet confessed. 'I played Viola for a week when Mrs Phillips was ill and I played Goneril. Oh, and I understudied Lady Capulet but I only got to play the part at a couple of matinées. I enjoy comedy, but managers only see me in dramatic parts.'

'You are certainly not the ingénue type,' Septimus Ryan agreed. 'Sir Henry, as one of the founders of this venture, what is your opinion?'

'I have no skill in the judgment of acting,' the silver-haired gentleman said, 'but I believe youth should be given its chance.'

'She's too tall to play second leads, distract attention from the leading lady,' Wendell Ryan said critically.

'We could use her in character parts, maids, walk-ons.'

'And have her help out as prompt or assistant wardrobe mistress,' his brother agreed. 'Are you handy with needle and thread?'

She nodded, aware that the job being offered her was far less than she had hoped, but also aware that she was not in a position to refuse anything.

'The full company has not yet been

mustered,' Wendell Ryan said. He spoke as if he were recruiting an army. 'However, if you are willing to accept a minor position in the company then we can offer you a place.'

At this point Nicholas would have hesitated, thrown into the air vague hints of parts he had been offered, and finally accepted with the air of doing them a great favour. Garnet said chokingly,

'I shall be happy to accept, sir.'

'Report here in a week's time for costume fittings and a read-through. I think Doll Tearsheet and the Nurse—and you can understudy Rosalind.'

It was as Orlando that she had first seen Nicholas when she had gone with the rest of the family to a performance at York.

'Miss Webber, perhaps you would do me the favour of taking a bite of supper with me in the greenroom?' the silver-haired man enquired.

Garnet frowned slightly. There were men who made a habit out of pursuing attractive young actresses, and actresses who made a habit of accepting. She had never been one of them. On the other hand she had told Nicholas that she was going out for supper and she had eaten little that day.

'Sir Henry is a most respected benefactor of the theatre,' Septimus Ryan said.

'Then thank you, sir. Provided I am not late,' she began.

'I'll have you taken home in good time, Miss

Webber. Shall we repair to the greenroom and enjoy something to eat?'

He was offering his arm with a slight bow. She laid her hand tentatively upon it, made her bow to the Ryan brothers, and went with him up the aisle to the foyer.

This was a small theatre, the conventional crimson and gold lightened by touches of white and pale blue. She looked round with pleasure. Although she had quickly learned the hardships of an actor's life she had never lost the thrill of being a part of the greasepaint and the flaring jets and the costumes sweaty from too many wearings.

'Beefsteak pie and a bottle of good champagne.' Sir Henry had paused to give orders to his servant. 'Some peaches too, if you can find any.'

The greenroom still carried traces of paint smell, and was remarkably neat.

'The birth of a new enterprise is always exciting,' Sir Henry commented. 'This theatre has been defunct for years, but a small group of us decided to open it up. The state of the theatre is not good, Miss Webber. Sensitivity of interpretation is sacrificed to spectacle, and the great classical works are ruthlessly chopped and mangled to suit the public taste—if you will excuse the term.'

'It's a laudable undertaking.' She peeled off her gloves and sat primly at the round table. It was not set so the supper invitation had not apparently been premeditated.

'Garnet Webber.' Sir Henry spoke her name thoughtfully. 'We haven't met before? When you were reciting the Lady Macbeth I fancied for a moment that I had seen you before.'

'I don't believe so, sir.' She paused as a man came in with napkins and cutlery, and began to lay the table.

'Thank you, George.' Sir Henry nodded a dismissal and gave a faintly sardonic glance in Garnet's direction. 'When one is immensely rich, my dear, one is generally well-served.'

'So it seems.' She watched the bearing in of the champagne in its icy bucket, the steaming pie with its golden crust, the dewy peaches.

'Help yourself.' He took the chair opposite her, giving the hot pie-dish a little push in her direction, waving manservant and waiter away.

'Ought we not to invite Mr Ryan and his brother?' she began.

'I can sup with Wendell and Septimus every day,' he returned. 'Help yourself, and then you can tell me what an obviously gently-reared young lady is doing earning her living on the stage.'

'It's an honourable profession!'

'But not always practised by the most honourable of people,' he said. 'You know, I was not lying when I said that you reminded me of someone. You don't hail from Yorkshire, I take it?'

'I might.' She spoke cautiously, the fear that

30

her mother might reach out to pull her back still strong.

'Webber. Garnet Webber.' He was not eating his own share of the meal.

'You have the advantage of me, sir,' she said lightly. 'I have not yet heard your own surname.'

'My dear young lady, I have been most impolite! The name is Ashton. Sir Henry Ashton.'

He stopped abruptly, recognition dawning in his face as it dawned in hers.

'Webber,' he said slowly. 'Dear Lord, but I ought to have recognised the name at once! You must be one of Fanny's girls.'

'And you are a kind of relation.'

'A distant connection, and by marriage only. My elder brother, Philip, eloped with your Aunt Esther. It was years ago. I understand there was a son.'

'Sabre. He owns Sabre Hall and the mill now.'

'My nephew. I had no idea there had ever been a child born of that marriage. Your other aunt, Gobnait, married my late wife's brother, Edward Grant. He died in Africa. My own wife died some years ago.'

'And you left Yorkshire.'

'I sold up and brought my daughter south. I didn't want the connection with the Sabres to continue. There has been an estrangement between our families since Esther and Philip ran off together all those years ago.'

'It's not talked about.'

'Well, it was a long time ago.' He poured some champagne and raised his own glass. 'This is a coincidence indeed. Perhaps we should drink to that.'

'To coincidence then.' She sipped the drink and smiled at him, her confidence growing. 'Have you never kept in contact? Surely it's not long since you left Ashton House?'

'I took Victoria away when Abigail died. I had been ill for quite a long time, heart trouble, gout, all the ills of middle age, and we hadn't visited Sabre Hall for years.'

'But you left Yorkshire when Abigail died. Why?'

'My dear, you are very young,' he began.

'Nineteen. I was thirteen when Cousin Abigail died. I'm not a child.'

'I am sixty-four. Anyone under forty seems remarkably young to me,' he said, smiling slightly. 'The truth is that when Abigail died your mother was good enough to warn me—'

'To warn you of what?' she asked sharply.

'My daughter, Victoria, had a somewhat romantic passion for Larch. I agreed with your mother that, as they were related, it would be wiser to separate them.'

'But not blood-related surely,' she protested.

'Perhaps not, but I hoped for a more suitable husband for my daughter than an illegitimate—'

'Larch was *my* blood kin and I was very fond of him,' she broke in.

'Call it an old father's foolishness if you like. I make no apology for it.'

'Did your daughter—?'

'Victoria is still unmarried. We have a large and comfortable house and we frequently travel abroad.'

His tone was dry but she sensed pain held in check.

'Larch married my sister, Pearl,' she said.

'I read about their deaths in that train disaster,' he said gravely. 'Believe me, but I bore Larch no personal animosity. I was sorry for him in many ways. It cannot be easy for a boy to grow up, knowing that he can never inherit the house where he was born. But I had Victoria to consider. Every father wishes the best for his daughter. I'm sure that your father did too.'

'He wanted us to be happy,' Garnet said simply.

'A sea-captain, wasn't he? I was pleased when I heard that Fanny had made such a successful second marriage. I have always had a great regard for your mother. Of all the Sabres she is the most admirable, and her first marriage was a most unhappy affair. I am not certain how much you have been told.'

'I know that Mother's first husband went off and lived with Aunt Gobnait,' Garnet said, 'and their daughter, Abigail, wed Cousin Larch.'

'It was very hard on Fanny,' Sir Henry said. 'Gobnait and Matthew Lawley lived together quite shamelessly in the same district, if you please. When he died I was glad to hear that Fanny had taken another husband. He never came to Sabre Hall?'

'We grew up in the States.' Garnet hesitated a moment, then said stiffly, 'I like Aunt Gobnait.'

'Oh, she always had spirit,' he allowed, 'but her conduct was very shocking. Elizabeth, my wife, died before Edward married her. He was something of an eccentric, but even so his marriage to Gobnait drove a further wedge between our two families.'

'Perhaps you would prefer me not to join the company after all,' Garnet said.

'I would like to know how Fanny's daughter comes to be acting on the public stage,' he said.

'Why, I'm continuing the scandalous tradition of the family,' she began, then shook her head. 'No, that sounds cheap and foolish! The truth is that I ran away. I fell in love with an actor and followed him to London. I've been working on and off ever since, and if that makes me unfit to associate with respectable people then so be it! I'm not ashamed of what I've done. I earn my living honestly and that's more than many can say!'

'You're not married?'

'No. No, I'm not married.' For a brief moment she looked defeated, older than her years.

'I am using some of my money to invest in what I regard as a cultural and laudable project,' Sir Henry said slowly. 'It is not part of my task to investigate the morals of those employed in the company. On the other hand you are the daughter of an old acquaintance of mine and I cannot avoid feeling a certain moral responsibility for you.'

'There's no need! I'm not your daughter.'

'But I have a regard for Fanny. She has always been—'

'The most admirable of the Sabres. You told me already.'

'I was going to say "a most excellent lady". I take it that she does not know your whereabouts?'

'She has never made any attempt to find me. I wrote to Aunt Gobnait and she's written to me twice, when Pearl and Larch were killed, and then when Grandmother Fausty died and Sabre inherited. Funny, but he's my cousin, and I've never even laid eyes on him.'

'And you have never written to your mother?'

'She could find me easily enough if she cared to take the trouble. I won't write to her.'

'And I don't intend to interfere,' he reassured her. 'However, if in time a

35

reconciliation could be effected, surely you would not object?'

She was silent for a long moment, her head bent, her fingers rubbing the bloom from a peach. The truth she refused to acknowledge was becoming clearer. There were days when she ached with longing for the moors, for the company of her sisters. Pretty, light-hearted Pearl was dead but there was still dear Rose with her limping gait. There was even a half-formed feeling that Fanny, in bribing Nicholas, might have genuinely hoped to spare her daughter pain.

'I don't know,' she said at last. 'I don't know anything any longer, but I'll not crawl home like a naughty little girl. I love Nicholas, you see, and I love the theatre too. He taught me to appreciate it. He really did. I won't leave him.'

'Nobody asks you to do anything.' He put his hand briefly over hers. 'In my opinion this young man ought to marry you, but you will tell me that this is none of my business. What I would like is to be your good friend, if you would not consider such an offer an impertinence.'

'I am not seeking another father,' she said.

'I already have a daughter,' he said. 'One is quite sufficient for an elderly man who still suffers from twinges of the gout.'

'I never spoke to Victoria, though I believe I saw her occasionally in the distance,' Garnet said. 'She seemed quite grown up.'

'Victoria is thirty-six, though she wouldn't thank me for revealing the fact,' Sir Henry said, smiling. 'She is certainly quite grown-up, though that's something a father finds hard to admit. Makes him feel old.'

'I don't think you seem so very old,' Garnet said impulsively.

'My health has certainly improved,' he said. 'I have widened my interests since I moved south. There is my Club, of course, and this new theatre project. I am full of plans and projects.'

She had the not entirely unpleasant feeling that she had just become another of them.

'I may write to my mother in a while,' she said, offering an olive branch. 'I would like to have a regular position in the company first though.'

'Fanny is a splendid woman,' he agreed, 'but nobody likes to hear "I told you so". Now, my dear Garnet, I am going to have George drive you home before your—friend begins to wonder where you are.'

'Oh, Nicholas will probably be asleep,' she said, aware of how bleak her words sounded.

'Well, here's my card. I hope you will do me the favour of calling—I am usually in during the mornings, and if I am not Victoria will be delighted to meet you.'

She wondered if age had mellowed him that he should begin to withdraw his objections to friendship with the Sabres, or if he were befriending her for th a sake of her mother for whom he clearly had a warm admiration. At least it was agreeable to have a friend and to have obtained, on her own initiative, a position in the new company. There had been little that was truly agreeable in her life for a considerable time.

CHAPTER THREE

Gobnait Sabre Grant finished reading through the letter for the second time, then folded it carefully and sat, frowning into the small fire that flickered on the hearth.

She was, as usual, in the kitchen of the small farm at Batley Tor which she had inherited from her lover, Matthew Lawley. Although the afternoon was warm she still lit a fire, having a love of heat engendered in her by the years she had spent in Africa with her husband, Edward Grant. Liza, her maid, was polishing in the big sitting room at the other side of the narrow hall. She could hear her humming as she waxed the floor and furniture. Gobnait preferred the homeliness of the kitchen with its scrubbed pine table, its rocking chair and the pots of herbs that lined the window sill. In this apartment she had known some of the happiest times of her life. Even without closing her eyes she could picture herself as she had been nearly forty years before, her red hair pulled back into a tail, her green eyes creased with laughter lines as Matthew interfered with her slapdash efforts at cooking. She could still feel his warm breath on her neck and smell the pungent, horsy smell mingled with bay that had been his own special scent. Oh, but she had been a fortunate woman. Those who prophesied that she would come to a bad end for stealing away her sister's husband had been wrong. She and Matthew Lawley had lived together for nearly fourteen years until his death. After that she had married her old suitor, dear, faithful Edward Grant, and shared his explorations in North Africa until his death.

Her return to Sabre Hall had been a mixture of joy and pain. It had been good to see her mother and Esther again but there had been the gap left by Abigail's sad death and the inescapable knowledge that, beneath her honeyed words of reconciliation, Fanny still hated her.

'Dear Aunt Gobnait,' Garnet had written, 'I am writing to assure you that I am in good health and have recently obtained a place in a new Classical Theatre company which has just been formed. You will never guess who is involved with its formation. Sir Henry Ashton! He spoke to me most kindly, saying that he wished, despite the coolness between our two families, to be my good friend. I did not like to enquire into the cause of the feud lest I inadvertently cause pain or embarrassment. Sir Henry seems to have a great admiration for Mother and would like us to be reconciled but I am very uncertain. The truth is that I miss you all very much but I'll not leave Nicholas, nor give up my place in the company. I wish that we could meet and have a long talk, for I have always felt you trusted me and I would value your advice.'

'Oh, Garnet!' Gobnait shook her head, speaking half-aloud. 'Garnet, what can I say to you? How can I possibly tell you the beginning of the affair, when Esther and Philip Ashton fell in love and Fanny confided to the Ashtons that there was insanity in the family? It wasn't true, but the Ashtons believed it and disowned Philip when he ran away with Esther. How can I tell you that our brother, Patrick, planned to marry the girl who was bearing his child and was murdered by a millhand he'd dismissed? That was what Fanny said, anyway, and she was the only witness! I can't talk to you of these things, Garnet. I don't have the right to put doubts in your mind, not when I was the one who stole your mother's husband away and bore him a child.'

'Did you call, Mrs Gobnait?' Liza, a cake of beeswax and a cloth in her hand, appeared in the doorway.

'I'm riding over to Sabre Hall,' Gobnait

said, rising. 'I'll be back before supper. You can cut some of the spiced beef and fry some potatoes.'

'Yes, ma'am.' Liza vanished again.

Riding was not only exercise for the body but relaxation for the mind. When she was in the saddle problems became small, easier to face.

The stables, from whence she derived most of her income, were built a little distance from the cottage. Gobnait knew and loved horses more than she knew and loved human beings. Sometimes she wondered, only half-humorously, if she had been a horse herself in some previous existence. There was certainly something equine in the toss of her head and the flare of her nostrils.

Between her breeched knees her mount responded to the pressure of her muscles, trotting, then cantering, down the steep hill that led to the farm. She relaxed into the rhythm, her lean, tall frame rising and falling, at one with the animal she controlled. An old person watching from a distance might have been deceived into believing she was her brother Patrick come again.

Rose, riding towards her, was too young ever to have known Patrick. Recognising her aunt, she waved her hand and drew rein as the older woman approached.

'I was coming to visit you,' she called. 'Are you coming to Sabre Hall?'

'Not if you're not at home,' Gobnait retorted. 'There's nothing wrong, I hope?'

'Nothing, save the usual argument over the Horse Show. Mother declares that she will not attend nor allow me to attend, and I wanted so much to see Sabre win all the prizes.'

'He'll not win them all,' Gobnait said, dismounting and giving her niece a leg down. 'I have entered several of the events myself, and don't go pulling down the corners of your mouth at me! I may be nearly sixty but I'm not ready for the chimney corner yet!'

'I wasn't saying anything,' Rose protested. 'I'd like to watch both you and Sabre compete.'

'Your mother has painful memories of the Show,' Gobnait said. 'It was on that day that your Aunt Esther eloped with Philip Ashton and on the very next day our brother Patrick was killed.'

'But that was years ago! Surely she cannot still mind,' Rose protested.

'Fanny has a long memory,' Gobnait said. 'She knows that one or two small events can change the pattern of many lives.'

'I believe that we make our own patterns,' Rose argued. 'Garnet has done so.'

'Garnet has written to me.' Gobnait fished out the letter and gave it to her.

'She's met Sir Henry Ashton!' Rose exclaimed after a few moments.

'I know. I read it.'

'I don't remember ever seeing him or his daughter,' Rose said. 'What relation is he exactly?'

'By blood, nothing. Esther married his brother and I married his wife's brother. The Ashtons never considered the Sabres to be of their class, unfortunately.'

'Perhaps Sir Henry is relenting.' Rose folded the letter and returned it. 'I hate old quarrels that don't mean anything any more!'

'That depends on who was involved in the original quarrel,' Gobnait said drily. 'It's easy to let bygones be bygones when one isn't the injured party. However, that doesn't concern you or Garnet.'

'It seems she is not married yet,' Rose said, with a quick, upward glance. 'Mother never mentions her name, but I know she feels the shame keenly.'

'And you imagine I will approve? Rose, Matthew Lawley and I could not have wed even if Fanny had agreed to a divorce. It would have been against the law. This Nicholas Brocklehurst has no such impediment in his life. He could make an honest woman of your sister at any time.'

'Perhaps Sir Henry will persuade them to it,' Rose said.

'Perhaps. I think we'll keep this letter to ourselves for a while. Garnet will decide what to do in her own good time.'

'And the Show? Are we to say nothing about

that either? I want very much to attend it.'

'To watch Sabre ride? You are very fond of him, aren't you?'

'Of course I am. He's my cousin.'

'Whose existence you never suspected until you met him when he came to Yorkshire. He was fortunate to find such loving relatives.'

'You're laughing at me,' Rose said reproachfully.

'A little, because you are so young. I cannot remember ever being as young as you are. Certainly I was never as pretty! You really are quite lovely. I hope Sabre finds it out.'

'Do you think he might?' There was no guile in the vivid face turned towards her. 'Oh, Aunt, do you think he might?'

'Men have done stranger things,' Gobnait said, smiling faintly. With all her heart she hoped that nothing would happen to take that look of trustful innocence from her niece's face. A marriage between her and Sabre would surely satisfy even Fanny's relentless ambition, and if Sabre were to fall in love then the marriage itself might be a happy one.

She remembered a certain far-off day when she and Esther, pale in her weeds, had walked together on the moor, and the latter had confided her secret.

'To you alone, Gobnait, lest anything ever happens to me. Philip and I had a son. He was born two months after Philip died of the fever. I've left him with the English nuns in Florence and later on I shall arrange for him to be schooled in Ireland. I've a little money for the purpose and the Irish uncles will help me. I called him Sabre. Sabre Ashton. He's six years old and I want to keep him safe until Mother dies and he comes to inherit. I want to keep him safe!'

Gobnait had not asked from whom. In both their minds had risen the memory of their brother Patrick, killed before he could wed his Irish sweetheart and give the child a legal surname.

'Why did you come back?' she had asked instead. 'Why didn't you stay in Italy to bring up Philip's son?'

'I couldn't endure to stay away from home a moment longer,' Esther had confessed, tears starting to her eyes. 'Oh, it wasn't too bad when Philip was alive. We had the prettiest villa and several of our neighbours spoke English, but I couldn't go on living there alone. Anyway Fanny might have begun to suspect something. You know how quick and clever she is.'

'And ruthless,' Gobnait had said.

'We don't know for certain,' Esther had said quickly. 'That drunken Joe Wilkins was hanged for the killing. All the evidence told against him.'

'And Patrick died before he could make an honest woman of his son's mother.'

'Larch is a nice little boy,' Esther said softly.

'Fanny is very fond of him you know. She makes an excellent mother.'

'And Larch will never be able to inherit. Even if Fanny were to bear a legitimate son, your child was born first.'

'But Fanny cannot bear a legitimate child now that Matthew is living with you,' Esther reminded her.

'It seems you have done better than any of us,' Gobnait grinned. 'Out of the four of us Fanny has no children, Patrick and I both produced bastards, and only you have carried on the succession. It seems a pity not to let Mother know, but she'd never be able to keep the news to herself, and you could hardly explain you wanted to keep the existence of your own child a secret for fear of what Fanny might do.'

That had been—Gobnait worked out a quick calculation in her head—thirty, thirty-one years before. Lord, but time flew while everything changed yet remained the same.

'Aunt?' Rose was tugging at her sleeve. 'Aunt, is anything wrong?'

'What? No, nothing. I was a long time off, that's all,' Gobnait said vaguely.

Thirty-one years, and now Matthew Lawley who had betrayed Fanny and made herself happy was as dead as the two men the sisters had later married, as dead as the bastard cousins Larch and Abigail, as dead as Pearl. Even Fausty, with her generous heart and the

46

brogue that had always set Fanny's teeth on edge, was gone. Out of the whole vibrant, quarrelling Sabre family there were only the three widowed sisters, the new owner of house and mill, Garnet far away in London, and this exquisite, limping child.

'If you are fond of Sabre,' Gobnait heard herself say, 'then make him wed you. Don't bury your nose in books until it's too late and he's caught another woman's cap. Make him see you as a desirable young woman and not the schoolgirl you were when he first came here.'

'How do I do that?' Rose asked.

'With a face like yours, that's not a question you need to be asking,' her aunt replied. 'Rose, I never had looks to match yours but two men once loved me more than they ever loved any other woman, and I want you to have something like that to remember when you're old yourself.'

'You're not old,' Rose said loyally.

'Old enough, but I've life in me yet.' Gobnait laughed and hugged her. 'Go and find Sabre. If you wheedle hard enough he'll persuade Fanny to let you attend the Show. This is your time, girl. You're in the morning of the rest of your life, so make it a sunny one.'

'And we'll not mention the letter?' Rose looked up at her.

'Not one little word. Your sister must manage her own affairs.'

'Poor Garnet! I cannot think what possessed her to run away and become an actress,' Rose said. 'She was never very interested in the plays of Shakespeare before.'

'I'd reckon she was more interested in the actor,' Gobnait said. 'Well, he may wed her and be knighted by the Queen, and then it'd make your head spin to see how quickly Fanny accepts the situation. Be off with you now and find Sabre—and remember what I told you. Any man can be caught if you've energy enough.'

'Mother would be pleased with me,' Rose said gravely. 'My lameness is a great trial to her.'

She mounted up again nimbly enough, gathered together the reins, and cantered away over the springing turf, her hair bobbing on her shoulders. Gobnait waved after her and continued to walk, her thoughts occupied with possibilities. If Sabre and Rose were to marry then much of the bitterness of the past and any likely dangers for the future would be obliterated. With a little shock she realised she had been worrying about what might happen if Sabre ever brought home a strange girl to be his wife.

Rose was enjoying her ride. In the saddle she felt free and graceful, lifted out of her normal, everyday self. She was not so expert a rider as Garnet, and even if she had been it wasn't likely that her mother would have allowed her to appear in a public competition.

'It embarrasses people when they see others less perfect than themselves flaunting their deficiencies in public,' Fanny had said. 'You'd not wish to cause embarrassment, would you?'

'Rose! Hey, Rose!'

The shout roused her from her abstraction and her recognition of the figure riding towards her lit her face into delight.

'Sabre, I thought you were in York,' she said.

'I'm on my way back. What have you been up to?' He slowed to a walk, wheeling his horse about to bring their two mounts together.

'Just riding. I saw Aunt Gobnait.'

'Riding too? This seems to be an afternoon for exercise.'

'I was hoping that she might think of some way of persuading Mother to let me attend the Horse Show,' Rose confided. 'I would like to see you and Aunt Gobnait win all the prizes.'

'Your mother never visits the Show, does she?' Sabre said.

'Oh, the occasion holds unhappy memories for her,' Rose said. 'And she does feel it on my account when we go into public. She finds it very hard indeed to have a crippled child.'

'That's nonsense—and you're not a cripple,' Sabre said roundly. 'I've never heard Aunt Fanny call you so, and I'll not allow you to use the term. Why, any man would be proud to appear in public with you at his side!'

'Would you?' She jerked sharply on her horse's rein, turning her face towards him. 'Would *you*, Sabre?'

'Yes. Yes, Rose, I would.' He too had drawn rein and his expression was gentle. 'You are a very lovely girl and, if you want to go to the York Show, then I'll take you. Aunt Fanny can scarcely object to my escorting my own cousin.'

'I'd not want to upset her,' Rose said.

'I think your mother is a tougher lady than you understand,' he smiled. 'From all that I hear she is not so easily upset. It's time you began to think of yourself and your own needs.'

'And, no doubt, Cousin Sabre will tell me what they are,' she said, her natural humour bubbling up.

'Naturally, if you cannot work it out for yourself,' he said solemnly, and smiled at her.

'The trouble is,' said Rose, twisting the reins between her fingers, 'that I'm all Mother has now. Pearl is dead and Garnet run off and I have been a disappointment to her since I was born.'

'That's nonsense,' he said again.

'Not really. Mother likes everything to be perfect, you see,' Rose said earnestly. 'She has never been able to bear deformities of any kind. Oh, you mustn't think that she is ever unkind. She is always very good, but it is not easy for her. She has always wanted the best for all of us, yet nothing has ever turned out

50

quite right for her. Pearl and Larch didn't have any children and then they were both killed in that awful train crash, and Garnet ran off after that actor; and now there's just me.'

'And what do you want for yourself?' Sabre asked.

'To be happy!' Her voice was suddenly intense, her blue eyes enormous. 'Oh, I want nothing save to be happy.'

'And going to the Show would make you happy?'

'It would be a beginning,' she said quaintly. 'It would be something!'

'I'll talk to your mother. Meanwhile I'll race you back to Sabre Hall,' he said.

'Done!' She spurred her horse into a gallop and was off across the moor before he could draw back. He watched her with pleasure, then started after her. He would give her a good chase and, at the last moment, allow her to win. There was something in his pretty cousin that brought out the gallantry in his nature.

Gobnait, having exercised her horse, was rubbing him down, a task she seldom left to the two grooms she employed. There was a soothing satisfaction in each long, sweeping stroke of cloth and curry comb. While she worked on the horse's velvety coat her own problems unravelled in her mind until they lay before her so clearly that she was able to begin working out a solution.

Her niece, Garnet, had, through the

intricate workings of what some people were pleased to call coincidence, become acquainted with Sir Henry Ashton. Sir Henry! She suppressed a smile, remembering long-past summers when the Ashtons and the Sabres had ridden, flirted and gossiped together. Henry had been the shy, solemn younger brother who had hoped to become a clergyman. Now he was a rich, elderly gentleman who spent his money in financing theatre projects, and who had clearly mellowed in his attitude to the Sabres.

'And he'd likely not recognise me these days either,' she said aloud.

The horse, hearing her voice, nuzzled her for sugar. She gave him one of the lumps she always carried in her pocket, and went out, breathing the comforting, familiar smells of hay and horse. If Henry took an interest in Garnet he might advance her career or make it worthwhile for Nicholas Brocklehurst to marry her. The thought that Nicholas Brocklehurst was not worthy of her niece brushed her mind but she shrugged it away. Unworthy husbands often created remarkably contented wives.

She gave the horse another lump of sugar and, hands thrust deep into her pockets, wandered back towards the cottage. She had had it repainted the previous year and the garden was doing well though she still hated weeding and put it off for as long as possible. The apple tree bore a quantity of ripening fruit. She looked up into its branches, remembering how often Abigail had crouched there, a book in her hands and dreams in her eyes. She had loved her daughter dearly and had been happy when she had married Larch. It had been hard to learn of her death, harder still to see her place taken by the shallow, silly Pearl.

'Supper's nearly ready, Mrs Gobnait,' Liza announced, appearing like a genie at the door. 'Was you wanting beetroot?'

'Beetroot would be splendid!' Gobnait approved, thrusting aside sadness. 'We'll both have it in the kitchen. I'm in a mood for company tonight!'

Rose, flying across the turf, glanced back to see her cousin pull rein in time to give her the added distance she required to win. It wasn't a gesture that hurt or annoyed her. Sabre was the kind of man who would always be kind. She was grateful to think that she had met such a man and that he seemed to be growing fond of her.

'Where in the world have you been?' Fanny, her voice sharp, had come to the door, her eyes on her daughter's untidy hair.

'You must blame me, Aunt.' Sabre had joined them. 'I bullied Rose into a race and we forgot the time.'

'Heavens, there's no blame.' Fanny's voice had warmed. 'I like to see young people enjoying themselves—but you must both be starved! I'll tell Maggie to hurry supper!'

CHAPTER FOUR

The invitation had been for afternoon tea, an occasion less informal than morning coffee and less important than dinner. Garnet couldn't avoid the suspicion that Victoria Ashton had invited her for the express purpose of looking her over. She could forgive the curiosity for she felt it in some measure herself. Sir Henry Ashton and his daughter had left the district at about the same time as Cousin Abigail had died and, prior to that, she had known Victoria only by sight, the former by reputation as an elderly invalid who seldom left his estate. The move south seemed to have afforded him a new lease of life. The gout had ceased troubling him and he displayed to Garnet only his most urbane and courteous facets. He was frequently at the theatre when the company met for rehearsals and she had run into him once or twice in the street.

'He thinks you're an absolute stunner, darling,' Nicholas said, lazily amused. 'The poor old boy hasn't any female companionship except his daughter, so he probably looks on you as his last chance to kick over the traces!'

'He's just being kind,' Garnet objected. 'I think he regrets the long estrangement between our families.'

'Why was there an estrangement in the first

place?' he enquired.

'I'm not sure. Apparently the Ashtons never thought the Sabres quite good enough,' she said. 'They objected to my Aunt Esther's marrying Sir Henry's brother and they were even more annoyed when Aunt Gobnait married his wife's brother.'

'Well, he's certainly mellowed,' Nicholas observed. 'I like his excuse for getting to know a pretty girl too! An interest in the Arts covers a multitude of sins.'

'He's genuinely interested,' Garnet protested.

'So you say.' Nicholas grinned. 'Oh, come on, my love! You don't really believe you got a job on your acting ability alone, do you? You're not exactly Sarah Siddons.'

'The Ryans employ me,' Garnet said, flushing. 'They're the managers.'

'And it's not likely they'd risk offending a patron,' he countered. 'Not that I mind. One of us has to pay the rent.'

'You'll get a job soon.'

'I'm not fretting. A rest is as good as a change.'

He spoke carelessly but she was not deceived. The truth was that Nicholas was not only far more talented than she would ever be, but he had a genuine love of the theatre that went deep as bone. Without any prospect of a part he became morose and careless, hiding his mood with jests that became progressively coarser.

'Well, whatever Sir Henry's motives,' Garnet said at last, keeping her tone cool and amused, 'as far as I'm concerned he makes an excellent substitute for a grandfather. I shall tell his daughter exactly the same thing if she asks me.'

'Better say "father", if you don't want to offend her,' Nicholas advised.

'It's natural that she should be curious,' Garnet said. 'We are connected by marriage and she has no other relatives save her father.'

'So you will sit and make polite conversation, eyeing each other like two—'

'There's no need to be rude,' she broke in.

'I was going to say like two beautiful ladies,' he said straight-faced.

'I am not beautiful,' Garnet said.

'You can give the impression of being so, and that's better.' He gave her an approving look.

'Thank you, kind sir.' She dropped him a curtsey and took up her parasol. 'I will see you later.'

'No rehearsal?'

'Not tonight, so I am at your disposal.'

'I'm sorry, sweetheart, but I have an engagement. If you'd let me know earlier I could have broken it, but as it is—'

'Cannot you break it?' she asked.

'Darling, if I could I would, but this is the semi-final of the billiards tournament. I can hardly let the other players down.'

'I suppose not.' She hid her disappointment under a smile. 'Try not to be too late.'

'Honour bright,' he said solemnly.

She blew him a kiss and went out jauntily. Today, with the rent paid up a month in advance, there was no need for her to scurry through the hall, and she further indulged herself by hailing a cab as soon as she reached the main street. Although the salary she was receiving was only a modest one it meant that she was no longer penniless, dependent on Nicholas's generosity.

The house to which Sir Henry had brought his daughter stood in a genteel square in one of the more expensive neighbourhoods. Paying the cabman, Garnet stood for a moment at the foot of the steps, looking up at the door with its elegant fanlight, the bay windows that overhung the railings. She was not absolutely certain but she fancied a lace curtain was twitched aside and then dropped.

At least she looked fresh and ladylike, though it was a pity she had only the new brown and cream outfit to wear. Sir Henry had already seen it several times.

There was a pause after the jangling of the bell and then the narrow, white door inched ajar and a liveried footman eyed her with a jaundiced air that brought the colour up into her cheeks.

'Miss Webber,' she said crisply, 'to take tea

with Miss Ashton.'

The footman silently stood aside and she entered a high-ceilinged lobby out of which a staircase curved steeply. The servant had closed the door and was preceding her up the stairs. She wondered if he had been instructed to carry his nose at that particular angle and stifled a giggle.

'Miss Webber.' The footman announced her and stood aside again.

Garnet had half-expected a roomful of people, but the white and gold apartment was empty save for the young woman who stood near the fireplace. The fashionable young woman, Garnet amended. Her dress was of pale amber silk, its tight bodice ruffled, its skirt drawn back into a frilled bustle. An ornament of peach roses was pinned in her blonde hair and a spray of matching roses decorated her bustle.

'Miss Webber, how good of you to come.' Victoria Ashton affected a languid drawl and limp handshake. She was certainly very pretty, her features regular, her complexion dainty, her figure a fashionable hourglass. With her bright curls, the little tinkling bracelet on her wrist, she would have passed for much younger than her years. Only the shadowed blue eyes and the creases that ran from nostrils to lip revealed middle-age.

'It was very good of you to ask me, Miss Ashton.' Garnet returned the limp handshake

58

with a firm one and took the chair indicated by the other.

Victoria Ashton returned to the fireplace where an elaborate display of gold and bronze roses filled the empty hearth. Posed thus, beneath the gilt-framed mirror, she made a charming picture. Garnet thought, with a touch of cynicism, that she probably practised it.

'We'll have tea. You do like tea?' She was tugging at a bellrope.

'Thank you.' Garnet inclined her head, wondering if the other had expected her to demand whisky.

'My father is at his Club, but that will give us time to gossip a little.' Victoria moved to another chair and seated herself. Whatever inclination she might have had to gossip had evidently died for she sat mute, her blue eyes fixed on Garnet as a maidservant came in with tea, toast and small, iced cakes.

'Thank you, Sarah.' Victoria gave a smiling dismissal. 'Will you take cream and sugar, Miss Webber?'

'A little.'

'You're fortunate to be so slender. I have to watch my waistline like a hawk.'

Victoria was making a pretty little ceremony out of pouring the tea.

'I've always been thin,' Garnet said with a touch of bluntness. 'My mother always said I never sat still long enough for flesh to make

59

any headway on my bones.'

'You have been in touch with her?' Victoria looked faintly surprised as she handed the teacup.

'I hear occasionally from Aunt Gobnait.'

'I am not acquainted with any of them,' Victoria said. 'My parents never wished it.'

'And you had no wishes of your own?' Garnet flashed her a level look.

'I knew Larch and Abigail very slightly,' Victoria admitted. 'She was younger than I, but I recall feeling a certain sympathy for her. As your aunt and Matthew Lawley were not received in the neighbourhood it followed that Abigail had no friends.'

'She had Cousin Larch. He married her,' Garnet said.

For an instant something bleak and tender flashed into Victoria Ashton's face. It vanished so quickly that Garnet thought she must have imagined it. Then the other said, 'I spoke to Larch once or twice. He seemed pleasant enough.'

'He was very pleasant,' Garnet said flatly.

'I was—sorry to hear of his death.' Again came the queer, bleak look. 'Your sister's too. My father and I read of it in the papers. We had, of course, left Yorkshire by then.'

'So had I.' Garnet shook her head to the proffered cakes. 'I was very sorry to hear of it too. Larch and Pearl were happy together, I believe.'

'One hopes so.' Victoria spoke somewhat brusquely. 'There has been a great deal of sadness in your family, from all that I hear.'

'Nearly as much sadness as scandal,' Garnet said boldly.

'As you so rightly say.' Victoria gave a cold little smile. 'Forgive me if I speak without tact but have you not added to the scandals by your ill-advised actions?'

'Because I ran away to go on the stage and now live with a man to whom I'm not married?'

'How frank you are!' Victoria set down her cup and saucer and dabbed her lips with a wisp of cambric.

'The word is shameless, Miss Ashton—or so the polite world calls it.' Two flags of scarlet unfurled across Garnet's cheekbones. 'However, it is my own affair. An invitation to tea is one thing. An invitation to a moral lecture is quite another!'

'You mistake my intention,' Victoria said quickly. 'I salute your independence. I have often considered women to be as capable of managing their own lives as men. However, it also occurs to me that a young lady in your situation must feel herself to be particularly vulnerable. I take it that the gentleman still wishes to marry you?'

'Of course he does! It is merely that certain considerations make it difficult.'

'Financial considerations?' Victoria put her

fingers together.

'The theatre is an exacting profession,' Garnet said.

'With the rewards small and slow in coming,' Victoria nodded.

'I suppose so.' Garnet had meant to keep cool and self possessed, but she could feel her face begin to burn again.

'Miss Webber, I hope you will allow me to speak as frankly as you have,' Victoria said. 'I am aware of your situation and, while applauding the courage that led you to shatter the conventions of polite society, I feel strongly that you ought not to be penalised.'

'Why should you care?' Garnet asked in astonishment.

'My own family and yours have been at odds for many years,' the other said. 'I would not presume to argue with my father's views, of course, but I cannot help feeling that I ought to do something to restore the balance. If it is only financial considerations which prevent your marriage, then you must allow me to help you.'

'I don't understand,' Garnet said blankly.

The other woman's smooth face showed a ripple of impatience.

'My father is an ageing man,' she said, 'and in many ways a lonely man. That makes him vulnerable. Men, even sensible men like my father, sometimes have foolish ideas. This is something I would like to prevent. I am most deeply attached to my father as, no doubt, you were to yours.'

'Sir Henry has been very kind to me,' Garnet began.

'And I intend to be even kinder,' Victoria said. 'I would be right, would I not, in supposing that your mother has broken off all communication with you?'

Garnet nodded silently.

'If you marry the young gentleman,' Victoria said, 'I shall be happy to provide your dowry.'

She spoke as calmly as if she had just offered her another cup of tea. The cup still in Garnet's hand shook slightly and she put it down hastily. This was not in the least what she had expected and, faced by the unexpected, she felt her defences crumble like chalk.

'There is no need,' she began, but Victoria Ashton was continuing as calmly as if she had not spoken.

'My father is a generous and indulgent man, and never enquires what I do with my allowance. When you and Mr Brocklehurst are married, I shall make you a private gift of three thousand pounds.'

'My mother paid Nicholas not to marry me,' Garnet said, choking over the irony.

'And he took the money?' There was a well-bred distaste in the other's voice.

'Why not? My mother should never have done such a thing,' Garnet said. 'Anyway we are not married!'

'But I hope that it will not be long before we are invited to your wedding,' Victoria said, smiling slightly. 'I keep my word, Miss Webber. The dowry will be yours on the morning of the ceremony.'

That was the moment when she ought to have risen, made some cleverly cutting remark, and swept out. Instead she found herself nodding her head slowly as if she were still in full command of her destiny.

'I look forward to receiving that invitation,' Victoria said. 'Will you have more tea?'

'Nothing, thank you.' Garnet rose somewhat shakily. 'I have to go home.'

'I'll have a cab called.' Victoria glided from the room.

It wasn't possible, Garnet thought. She couldn't possibly be sitting in this elegant white and gold drawing-room having just received the offer of a bribe from a woman terrified lest her father be caught in the toils of an unscrupulous woman.

'The cab will be here in a moment,' Victoria said, returning. 'I shall tell Papa that you came to drink tea and that I find you a most congenial companion. When does the Season begin?'

'Season?'

'The theatrical season. When is the first performance?'

'In three weeks. We are putting on

"Volpone" first. I don't have a part in that.'

'Then I've no doubt that you will be granted a few days' leave of absence, for the honeymoon.'

'Do you always get exactly what you want?' Garnet asked with a spasm of irritation.

'Not always.' The other's face showed every year of her age. 'Not always, Miss Webber.'

She moved away and stood by the window, looking out into the square.

The footman, as lofty and impenetrable as before, showed Garnet out and assisted her up to the vehicle.

Nicholas was not in the apartment. Garnet took off her hat and looked round the littered room with distaste. She had left it in a state of reasonable neatness, but he had contrived to untidy it again before leaving. His soiled cravat was flung over the back of a chair, the bedcovers were rumpled, a cup of cold coffee was on the table, and there was a layer of scum on the water in the ewer. She had endured this for two years and the thought came to her that she wouldn't be able to endure it for very much longer. Without a part or the promise of one, Nicholas was rapidly becoming slovenly. Away from the stage the dark flame of his personality flickered and shrank.

She set about tidying the room, her thoughts elsewhere. Nicholas intended to marry her. He had said so often and it was only circumstances that had prevented it. Once married their luck would change and a way paved for reconciliation with her family. She was beginning to realise how much she missed them.

It was a pity there was no rehearsal to keep her mind occupied during the evening. She changed her formal dress for a rosy dressing gown with marabou on collar and cuffs, combed out her long hair, sprayed perfume. That she was acting like a woman uncertain of her lover's affections occurred to her but she dismissed it. Nicholas would have eaten his supper. She grated an apple, forced herself to eat some bread and butter. The evening was warm, the strip of sky still dappled with sunlight, but she lit the fire and trimmed the lamps. When Nicholas did come home it would be to a welcome.

Later she sat by the window, shielded by the curtain, listening to the city as it prepared for the night. At Sabre Hall there had been only the wind across the moor, the muted whinny of horse in stable. Here there were urchin cries, two quarrelling voices from next door, the rattling of wheels over cobbles and, beyond those sounds, the dull roar from roads and alleyways.

Nicholas was not late. It was scarcely ten when she heard his steps below. He was not foxed either. His voice, clear and unslurred, rang through the doorway.

'Put the kettle on, sweetheart! We've

something to celebrate.'

'You won the semi-final.' She rose to kiss him, her pink gown swirling.

'Naturally. Did you doubt it?' He put his arms round her, holding her tightly. 'We'll have some punch. Do you have lemons?'

'There's one in the cupboard.'

'That will do. Bring the nutmeg. I've more than a billiards score to celebrate.'

'A part?'

Nothing less could have brought such a glow to his dark eyes.

'A better-than-even chance of one. Mind you, its in the provinces but the company will very probably come to London eventually.'

'Where in the provinces?' Her own voice was muted, but he didn't seem to notice.

'Oh, Birmingham, Newcastle, Coventry,' he said vaguely. 'I'll be playing leads.'

'And travelling.'

'We'll both be travelling,' Nicholas said, bringing down the pewter mugs. 'You don't think I'll be leaving you to your own sweet devices, do you?'

'But I shall be working myself,' she reminded him.

'You'll have to give in your notice,' he said.

'Nicholas, I can't! I can't give in my notice three weeks before we open!'

'Sweetheart, the roles you play are so tiny that almost any competent actress can replace you,' he said.

'At least they pay the rent,' she said, hurt by his careless tone. 'And these leading parts in the provinces are not yours yet.'

'I audition next week,' he told her.

'Then you won't object if I hold onto my own tiny parts for a while longer?' She was unable to keep the sarcasm from her voice.

'You wouldn't want to stay here without me, would you?' He spoke coaxingly, stirring the fragrant punch as the bubbles broke the surface.

'We're not wed.' Garnet accepted her tankard, blew on it gently, her long lashes downcast.

'Dear heart, we couldn't be more married if we were married,' he said smilingly. 'Why the sudden craze for respectability? Are you afraid you'll be cut out of the family fortune?'

'There isn't any,' she said. 'My cousin owns the house and mill and my mother takes a percentage of the profits for working there. She's managed the business for years. What money she had from her second marriage was for my sisters and me, but Pearl was killed and I am estranged, so I suppose Rose will get the little that is left.'

'And as I never have any money, we shall have to live in single blessedness until the end of the story.'

'You'd not marry me else?'

'Not until I can afford to keep you in a manner befitting a well-bred young lady. Drink

68

your punch, darling.'

She drank obediently, the heat of it stinging her eyes.

'Nicholas, if we did marry there would be money,' she said at last.

'The Lord will provide, I suppose. Garnet, you're a beautiful optimist!'

'Victoria Ashton will provide,' Garnet said.

'What?' Nicholas stared at her.

'I went for afternoon tea if you remember,' she said, 'and she was very agreeable. She regrets the long feud between our two families and wishes to be our friend.'

'And how does she propose to do that?'

'She proposes to give me a dowry of three thousand pounds,' Garnet said.

'Whew!' Nicholas set down the tankard and stared at her.

'When we marry.'

'Darling, you must be a genius! How did you contrive it?' he demanded.

'I didn't. Miss Ashton offered,' Garnet said.

'Sweetheart, will you do me the honour of accepting my hand in marriage?' he said promptly.

He was smiling and his arms held her warmly but she felt, even as she accepted, a silent weeping at the thought of how it might have been.

CHAPTER FIVE

Rose was still finding it difficult to believe that she was actually at the Show. It was several years since she had visited the event and it seemed to her as she sat, primly excited, in her reserved seat with Aunt Esther that the Show had been going on without pause ever since. The same gypsy waggons, painted yellow and scarlet and turquoise, were circled up in the lower meadows. The same solemn-faced children were trotting their ponies round the ring, and she could have sworn that exactly the same cakes were being sold from the refreshment tent.

'You know, my dear, I am rather pleased that I agreed to come,' Esther said in her gentle way. 'I have always quite dreaded this particular day. I ran away with Philip Ashton on this occasion while the rest of the family came to watch the events. Oh, it was a most happy marriage, but I fear it caused a great deal of trouble. And it was on this day that poor Abigail died—but perhaps we ought not to dwell on past unhappiness.'

'Today is going to be a lovely day,' Rose said serenely. 'The prizes that Sabre doesn't win, Aunt Gobnait will take home.'

'They are both splendid riders, aren't they?' Esther said, watching them as they saddled up

70

in the enclosure. Grey head and dark red head were together and their profiles had the same aristocratic sharpness.

'They are bound to win!' Rose exclaimed, clasping her hands together tightly.

'It is a pity that Fanny could not feel able to come,' Esther said with genuine regret. 'I am certain she would have enjoyed it.'

Rose said nothing. To her secret shame she was rather relieved than otherwise that her mother had decided against coming.

'I really don't feel able to cope with the flood of memories the occasion releases,' Fanny had said. 'However, your Aunt Gobnait is by no means an adequate chaperone in view of her own history.'

She spoke as if Matthew Lawley had been dead for only a brief time instead of twenty years.

'I will be perfectly safe with Cousin Sabre,' Rose had begun.

'One hopes so indeed. Certainly he has always displayed the instincts of a gentleman despite his somewhat unorthodox upbringing,' Fanny allowed, 'but you are a young lady now and it would be most unseemly for you to appear with him in public without a respectable chaperone.'

Rose refrained from pointing out that she and Sabre frequently rode together unaccompanied. Permission to attend the Horse Show had been grudgingly given as it was, and she feared lest it be withdrawn.

'Esther will have to go with you, that's all,' Fanny said a last. 'Sabre will be riding, I suppose, so Oldfield had better take you both.'

That meant riding in the stuffy carriage instead of bowling along in the trap. Rose stifled a sigh and nodded obediently. Aunt Esther left the confines of Sabre Hall so seldom that this visit would be a treat for her.

She certainly looked as if she were enjoying herself. There was a glow of pink in her cheeks and she was almost girlish in her smiling.

'The jumps are higher than when I was young,' she was observing. 'I never took part myself, of course, but Patrick and Gobnait always competed and the Ashton boys. Edward Grant too. He and Gobnait had a running contest, year after year, as to who would bring home the blue ribbon.'

'I'll wager on Sabre,' Rose said. 'He'll win.'

'Five pounds on Gobnait,' Esther returned, 'and don't tell your mother!'

They laughed together like a couple of conspirators. Overhead clouds scudded across a hot blue sky and the wind was warm. Sabre was mounted now, his long legs gripping the horse he rode, his head burnished by the sun. Rose thought that, whether he won or not, he was the handsomest man in the Show. She watched avidly as he positioned himself ready for the starter's flag. There was an exquisite pleasure that was part pain in watching him gather himself ready for the jump off, holding her breath as the seconds ticked by. There was always the possibility that he might take a fall or be a couple of seconds behind one of the other competitors. Mounted, hands gripping the reins, he was at one with the beast he rode, his long, lean back slightly bowed, his lashes tipped with gold. She sat as still as he, waiting.

Fanny had the house to herself, Maggie having gone into the village for the afternoon to see a friend. It was so rare an event to have complete privacy that she savoured it for an hour or two like a child with a new toy. She made herself a light lunch of soup and salad, and in defiance of one of her most stringent rules, ate it from a tray with a book propped up before her. The house folded itself round her and she was lapped in a quietness her restless nature seldom knew. Her meal finished, she carried the tray out to the kitchen and washed up the dishes. The day was so warm and sunny that she was tempted into the garden, not to trim or weed, but to sit for half an hour in unaccustomed idleness.

She had sat for no more than ten minutes, however, before conscience brought her to her feet again. Her own pony was in the stable and needed exercise. She welcomed the notion of a little exercise herself.

Twenty minutes later, clad in her habit of black broadcloth with a snowy white jabot, she was cantering towards Batley Tor. It was seldom that she visited the stud farm for, of all places, it held the most painful memories for her. It was at Batley Tor that Gobnait and Matthew Lawley had lived together in defiance of every convention and reared their bastard. It was at Batley Tor that her brother Patrick had met his death. Her mind shied away from details of that and she fixed her thoughts instead on the pale, plain girl who had induced Patrick's son to marry her. There had been nothing she could do to prevent that marriage. She had been in America, embarked upon a second marriage and the bearing of three daughters. Not until her return had she been able to set the wheels in motion that would free Larch and enable his marriage to her own girl, Pearl, to take place. In that, at least, she had been successful. It was not her fault that they had chosen to travel on a train which was destined to crash; nor could she have foreseen that Esther's son should have turned up out of the blue to claim everything she craved eventually for herself and her descendants.

There was no reason for her to come here at all, but she felt that it might be interesting to take a look at the place. Gobnait had never cared much for housework and gardening, and it would be instructive to see how run down the farm had become.

Rather to her disappointment the garden

was reasonably tidy, the house fairly well-repaired though her sharp eye noted a couple of loose slates and a peeling of paint on the window sill. She tethered her horse at the gate, went up the path and rang the bell. There was no answer to the jangling. Gobnait had probably taken young Liza with her. Fanny put her hand to the knob and twisted it. As she had expected the door opened easily. It was typical of Gobnait to go off for the day and neglect to lock up!

She entered the narrow passage and turned into the large drawing room. The original parlour had been extended and an extra bedchamber built above. This room was clean and polished but no attempt had been made to impart any touch of femininity to it. There were horse brasses on the walls and several sporting periodicals were piled on a table. Gobnait had never cared for what she called 'frills and fripperies', yet two men had loved her devotedly until their deaths.

There were several letters in the wooden rack. Fanny rifled through them swiftly. A receipted bill for feed, a brochure advertising a new type of halter, a note from the veterinary surgeon to remind her that he was due to make his rounds the following week, a letter in Garnet's hand. It had been opened and left where anyone might read it.

She took out the single sheet of paper, unfolded it and read.

'Dear Aunt Gobnait,

I write as usual to you because I know you will respect my desire for privacy. I hope that you are well and that the stud farm continues to prosper. I hope also that they are all well at Sabre Hall. I have news of my own which I would like you to keep to yourself for the moment though I propose to write to Mother in a month or two. First, let me assure you that I am in excellent health and have joined a new company which has been formed for the purpose of reintroducing a more classical flavour to the present London repertoire. One of the patrons of the venture is none other than Sir Henry Ashton. He and his daughter, Victoria, live now in London and have been most kind to me. Sir Henry is a fine looking man, not in the least the grouchy invalid one might imagine. He is also immensely rich and their house in Bloomingdale Square is a fine one. Now for my most exciting piece of news— at least it is exciting to me! Nicholas has invited me to be his wife and I have accepted. I know you will be pleased and I hope that when I write to Mother the news will pave the way for an eventual reconciliation. Nicholas has the opportunity of playing provincial leads but may wait until a better opportunity offers. Thanks to the generosity of Miss Victoria Ashton we are not in immediate financial need. The wedding itself is to be a very quiet one. I have not even told Sir Henry that it is to take place. Victoria feels that he might be disturbed by it, a notion which makes me smile, for though he has been most helpful he is certainly too old to entertain any romantical notions about me! Write to me soon, my dear Aunt, and regale me with all the gossip. As soon as I am respectably wed I will write to Mother and Rose. Perhaps we will be able to visit all of you quite soon. Meanwhile I know that you will wish me happy and send your good wishes to us both.

Your loving niece,
Garnet.'

Fanny read the missive through twice, folded it again neatly and put the letter back into the rack. Nobody would have been able to guess from the calmness of her face that she was torn apart by the most furious anger. So Garnet hoped to pave the way for a reconciliation by throwing herself away on the wastrel whom she had followed to London! A lovely, high-spirited girl who might have had her choice of suitors had flung her chances out of the window! That there were very few eligible young men in the district didn't, at that moment, weigh in her considerations. Garnet had defied her and now, instead of coming back to beg forgiveness, she was planning to marry the man who had shamed her. And she was apparently going to marry with the financial help and support of Victoria Ashton!

Fanny sat very still, remembering a far-off

77

day when Philip Ashton, whom she had loved, had confided that he intended to marry her sister, Esther. So much had happened since that moment. So much loving and hating, so many schemes. Henry Ashton, the shy young man who had once hoped to enter the Church, had become implacable in his dislike of the Sabre family. He had married Elizabeth Grant, once Esther's best friend, and their only daughter, Victoria, had never been allowed to mix with the Sabres. Fanny had spoken to her only after she had grown up, and found her a sensible, attractive girl who would never allow her heart to rule her head. It seemed that Victoria had not changed either. Fanny had not missed the subtler implications of what her daughter had written. Obviously she feared lest her father was about to make a fool of himself with a younger woman and, if Victoria feared that, then clearly she had reason. Garnet had it in her power to become Lady Ashton, a prospect she blithely ignored in favour of Nicholas Brocklehurst!

Fanny sat still for a while longer, her mind making and discarding various plans. Only when she was quite certain what she intended to do did she rise, make her way out of the cottage, and ride home again. The anger had gone, replaced by a cool and steely determination.

Sabre had won the coveted blue ribbon with Aunt Gobnait only two points behind him.

Palms tingling from the vigour of her clapping, Rose sat bolt upright, bright spots of colour in each cheek. With her blunt cut black hair feathering her forehead and brilliantly blue eyes she had the look of an exquisite Dutch doll. Sabre, accepting congratulations and a challenge for the following year, thought not for the first time that his cousin was a lovely girl. Not only lovely in face, but gentle in nature. There were times when he suspected that her mother was not as kind to her as she might have been.

'Did you enjoy it?' He ducked beneath a rope, signalling Oldfield to take his horse.

'It was magnificent!' Esther cried with enthusiasm. 'I was saying to Rose that I was not sure if I should have come but now I am glad that I did. You and Gobnait were simply splendid!'

'It was a close contest,' Sabre allowed. 'Are you coming for some refreshments?'

He addressed both of them, but Esther shook her head.

'I'll wait for Gobnait,' she said, 'but Rose will be wanting something.'

'Come on, Rose.' He held out his hand to her as if she were still a child, and was surprised when she rose, tilting her chin, and said with dignity, 'I am not hungry, but I would appreciate a glass of wine.'

'Wine then.' He was not sure she was allowed to drink wine but let the matter pass.

They walked, side by side, across the field that sloped down towards the river.

'It's so hot in the refreshment tent,' Rose said.

'I'll bring a glass out to you.' He quickened his step, hurrying among the crowd, half a head taller than most of them.

There were benches here and there set under trees. Rose seated herself, smoothing down her skirt, feeling pleasantly grown-up. There were not many who had such a distinguished escort. The tiny part of her attention that was not occupied with Sabre had already noted the languishing glances of certain young ladies. As far as she could tell the glances had not been returned.

'Here's your drink.' Returning, Sabre held out the glass to her. 'What are you looking so serious about?'

Not expecting the question, she answered without stopping to think. 'Oh, I was wondering what kind of girl you liked.'

'Ones with black hair and blue eyes,' he answered with easy gallantry.

'I meant it seriously,' she said, hurt.

'I answered seriously.' To his surprise he found that he meant it. Seated next to her on the wooden bench he could smell the lavender cologne she wore, and see, beneath the little straw bonnet, the frail white neck where the heavy wings of hair parted. There was something restful about her, something that was of a very different quality from what he usually sought and found in the opposite sex.

'You're very flattering,' she said, and drank her wine quickly, wishing that she was older and didn't blush so readily.

'With you I don't flatter.' He raised his glass, smiling at her. 'With you I can speak the truth.'

'Men only say that to women who are either very old or very young,' she chided.

'Well, I see no grey hair.' His amused gaze travelled slowly over her face.

'I am not a child either,' she said stiffly.

His eyes had roved past the small, square chin and slender throat to the breasts that thrust upward against the silk of her bodice.

'No.' His voice had changed, imperceptibly roughened and thickened. 'No, you're not a child, Rose. It's honest to God true that you're not that!'

Her cheeks were pinker than ever and there was the dawning in her face of something that might blossom or wither as the days of her life wore on. The man who watched her was touched by her innocence, stirred by that promise of something more.

'Sabre, did you ever think of settling down?' she asked breathlessly. 'I mean, of marrying someone and of—of raising a family?'

'I've always been a wanderer.' For moment his gaze was sombre. 'Italy, then Ireland, other places where I generally end up making a fool of myself.'

'But you've a home now. You have Sabre Hall and the mill,' she reminded him.

'And you think I need heirs to whom I can leave it?'

'I don't have any right,' she said, shyness claiming her again, 'to interfere in your affairs.'

'Dear Rose!' He took the glass from her and set it with his beneath the bench. 'Dear Rose, you can say anything you like to me. Anything in the world! Do you really think I ought to settle down and take a wife?'

'I suppose so.' She felt herself trembling as his hand tilted her chin.

'And will you choose one for me?' he asked.

'Surely you know lots of ladies!'

'Too many, and I can't think of any offhand whom I'd care to bring as mistress to Sabre Hall. Choose me a wife, cousin.'

To her embarrassment tears stung her eyes. He was teasing her again as if she were a child.

'Choose me a wife,' he repeated. 'Choose me one with black hair and blue eyes who is neither too old nor too young.'

'Sabre?' Her voice was no more than a whisper.

'Would you consider me as a husband?' he asked lightly. 'I am too old for you, of course.'

'Oh, no!' She put up her small hand to his mouth. 'Oh, you are in the very prime of life. Gentlemen wear much better than women.'

'And you with your vast experience would know, I suppose?'

'Sabre, don't joke,' she pleaded.

'Darling cousin, if we were alone in the moonlight instead of in a crowded meadow I would do all the proper things,' he assured her. 'I will ask you in the most romantic manner that was ever devised when the surroundings are more propitious, but you must give me some hint of your answer now. A man doesn't like to make a fool of himself.'

'I wouldn't let you do that,' she said gravely.

'Not let me ask or not let me make a fool of myself?' he enquired.

'If you were to ask,' she said softly, her eyes still on his face, 'I would not make a fool of you, but my mother would have to give her permission.'

'When the moonlight comes then.' He took her hand, uncurling her fingers, kissing the tingling palm.

'And I will give you your answer then, if my mother agrees.'

'I rather fancy that she will.'

If there was a touch of cynicism in his voice the girl didn't notice it. She was in that state when it is scarcely possible to believe in an unexpected happiness, when one fears to breathe lest the moment be shattered.

'Ah, there you both are!' Gobnait, still in breeches which she preferred to divided skirts, strode towards them. 'Sabre, do see if you can

83

get a couple of hot pies. The crush in that refreshment tent is awful! Esther met up with an old friend—Arabella someone or other. Fat girl when I knew her and she's still fat.'

Her arrival was not resented. Rose felt she needed time in which to catch her breath. Sabre was in the throes of wondering what had possessed him to speak of marriage on impulse when he had spent his life avoiding entanglements.

'I'll find something to stave off the pangs,' he said, relinquishing his cousin's hand.

Gobnait, on whom the kiss had not been entirely lost, took his place on the bench, shot her niece a shrewd glance, and said merely,

'Well, this is turning out to be quite a day! Sabre rides beautifully, but if I were ten years younger I'd have given him a run for his money. Have to be starting back soon or Fanny will worry. She's been alone all day.'

'I know.' For almost the first time there was no guilt in Rose's voice.

Gobnait shot her another look, but refrained from comment. Love, she thought, must be given time to grow. It couldn't be forced against its will, nor prevented once it had begun. To this marriage there would be no objection. Fanny would be delighted and the future of the property would be assured. She reached over and patted her niece's hand in a rare gesture of affection.

Fanny had ridden home in a leisurely

fashion, attended to the needs of her horse, changed her clothes and was setting the table for supper when she heard the carriage lumber down the winding track. She went to open the door, holding it wide, her smile serenely welcoming.

'Esther, you look chilled to death. Come to the fire at once.' Her voice was anxiously chiding. 'I hope you have not been sitting about in draughts!'

'Fanny, it was hot,' Esther protested mildly.

'It's chilly now. No sign of Maggie, I suppose? She'll have lingered to gossip. Oldfield, you'd better drive on down to the village and pick her up. She cannot walk back after dark.'

'Horses need a bit of a rest,' Oldfield said, clambering down.

'You mean you'd like a bit of a rest, don't you?' Fanny said. 'Very well. Ten minutes and then start off if she's not back. Rose, why are you hanging about my heels?'

She rounded upon her daughter who had lingered behind Esther.

'Sabre won the blue ribbon,' Rose said.

'I guessed that he would. He rides like my brother used to do,' Fanny said, pleased.

'Aunt Gobnait was only two points behind,' Rose said.

'At her age she'd have displayed more dignity if she'd remained a spectator,' Fanny said. 'Close the door, dear. You're letting in the night air.'

'Sabre's following behind,' Rose informed her.

'Well, he'll very likely go straight to the stable and come in the back way.'

'I had a very good time today.' Rose closed the door reluctantly.

'Did you? You stayed with your aunt and didn't make a spectacle of yourself?'

'I stayed with Aunt Esther.' Some of the eager, confiding look in the girl's face had faded.

'This is not a day of happy memories for me, but I'm glad you enjoyed yourself,' Fanny said in a softer tone. 'Go and take off your bonnet and cloak. We'll have supper soon.'

Perhaps it was as well to say nothing until Sabre had made a proper declaration. Rose, making her slow way upstairs, felt the excitement of the afternoon bubble up in her again. Sabre had kissed her hand and, when he had raised his head, his grey eyes had lingered on her mouth. A shiver ran through her. She was innocent but, despite all Fanny's precautions, not entirely ignorant. What Sabre did with the women he knew but would not marry was not entirely clear. Ladies, she had been told, did not enjoy such activities. Rose suspected that she might enjoy them very much indeed.

Esther, obediently warming already warm hands at the fire in the drawing room, turned as her sister came in.

'It was very good of you to let Rose go today,' she said gratefully. 'She enjoyed herself immensely. You will never guess who I met there. Do you remember Arabella Atkin that was? She is Arabella Dowson now.'

'Is she still fat?' Fanny enquired with interest.

'Fatter,' Esther said, giggling.

'Well, we're all getting older,' Fanny said.

'Sabre rode well.' Esther hesitated, then said, 'I believe he has a certain *tendresse* for Rose. You would not object?'

'I would like it above all things,' Fanny said, her face brightening. 'However, the matter will have to wait for a few weeks. I am forced to travel to London almost at once.'

'To London? Why?' Esther asked in surprise.

'There is an exhibition of new dyeing methods in the city,' Fanny said. 'Much richer, darker colours are coming into fashion and we need to move with the times if we are to keep up the level of profits. Also I have a few shares that need to be looked into while I'm there. I shall be away for about a week, I expect.'

'Will you be—?' Esther hesitated.

'I shall go alone. You can surely contrive to manage here while I am away?'

'I was going to ask,' Esther said, gathering together her courage, 'if you intended to seek out Garnet. You know that she writes occasionally to Gobnait? It would be easy enough for you to discover where she is living.'

Her voice died away uncertainly as she saw the other's face.

'Garnet made her bed and must learn to lie on it,' Fanny said. 'I don't intend to seek her out without invitation.'

CHAPTER SIX

Fanny had not been in London for several years and, though her errand was an unwelcome one, she felt a small glow of pleasure as the train left the station at York. Nobody at home had questioned her sudden decision to leave on a trip. Nobody ever did question Fanny, and her tale of visiting the exhibition was accepted. She had, in fact, ensured from a brief perusal of the newspaper that an exhibition was, quite genuinely, taking place. She would make it her business to attend.

Her daughter, Pearl, and Larch had been killed in a train disaster. The memory of their tragic deaths two years before touched her mind briefly, but she felt no twinge of superstitious fear. Travel was becoming safer all the time. Fanny, who had accompanied her second husband on several of his voyages, settled back comfortably in her corner seat, fixed a woman who looked as if she might enter into conversation with a quelling glance, and opened her book.

She had written to reserve a room at a modest hotel where solitary ladies were accommodated in respectability and comfort, and now three days later she was ready to embark on a mission which would, she guessed, require all her skill. She had made her plans and now, as her eyes scanned the printed pages of her book, her mind ran through the actions and the talks she intended to take and have during her sojurn in the capital.

'I will be back before the week is out.' She had kissed Rose, noting with pleasure that the girl was wearing one of her prettiest gowns. Clearly she was in love. Rose was usually more interested in books than dresses.

'Aunt Esther and I will be perfectly all right,' Rose had assured her. 'Sabre will be here.'

It had crossed Fanny's mind that if Esther were an inadequate chaperone at the Horse Show she was scarcely likely to prove more efficient when Sabre was actually sleeping in the same house. However, a certain laxity in the atmosphere might prove a spur to his passion. The idea pleased her.

The train drew in at last and she rose, stretching her cramped limbs, preparing to meet the noise and bustle of the crowded platform. A porter, alerted by her look of authority, took charge of her small trunk and escorted her to a cab. Sitting bolt upright on the upholstered seat she watched the passing people with casual interest. It was unlikely that she would see Garnet amid the hurrying crowd, but she couldn't avoid a certain curiosity as to whether the girl had changed since she had run away. It would have afforded her a certain wry satisfaction to see her daughter rendered cheap and painted by the irregular life she led. The pity of it was that she dared not risk meeting her at all.

The hotel had received her letter and the manager, remembering from a previous visit that she was exacting but generous with her gratuities, personally escorted her to her bedchamber.

'Where I am sure you will be most comfortable, Mrs Webber,' he said. 'Will you require a meal in your room or would you prefer to eat in the dining room?'

'Up here. I have business tomorrow and intend to retire early.' She dismissed him briskly and pleasantly and turned to her unpacking with the air of a woman who knows exactly what she is about.

Morning found her rested after a peaceful night's sleep, her hair smoothed down under a small grey toque trimmed with black, her slender figure encased in a grey suit with a blouse of black voile. The outfit had the air of mourning muted but not obliterated by time.

She drank the coffee she had ordered, read through the two newspapers she had bought, with more intention of passing an hour than from any expectation of finding any announcement of Garnet's forthcoming marriage. Unless Garnet was already married? That question brought a frown to her brow but, after a moment, she shook her head, impatient with her own lack of confidence. Garnet was still under age and a marriage made could also be a marriage broken.

It was nearly eleven o'clock before she emerged from the hotel and began to walk slowly but purposefully in the direction of Garnet's lodgings. The girl had been naive to put the address at the head of her letter to Gobnait. Certainly it was not a good address, though she had evidently not yet sunk to the depths of Seven Dials and Flower Street.

At this hour, if what she had read about the habits of theatricals was accurate, Garnet would be at rehearsal if she were employed in a company. Nicholas Brocklehurst was far more likely to be at home. He had looked, Fanny thought with a spasm of dislike, like a man who kept irregular hours.

She stopped dead, seeing the tall graceful figure stride out across the street in front of her. They were no more than ten yards apart but Garnet went by without even turning her head. Even in profile her features were unmistakable. Her hat and gown were modish, her hair rolled into an elaborate pleat, and Fanny suspected, though she could not have sworn, that there was paint on her lips. Something more potent than anger shook her. This was Garnet, elder of her two surviving daughters, who had been such a quaint, long-legged little girl when her father was alive. She should have been richly married, not living in this drab neighbourhood, scratching a living by displaying herself on the public boards.

She was gone. Fanny shook off the misery that had gripped her and walked with renewed purpose up to the railed steps of the terraced house. The front door, with its panes of cheap coloured glass, yielded to her touch; a row of letter boxes informed her that Mr and Mrs Brocklehurst—pray God that was merely a sop to convention!—lived on the first floor.

The carpet on the staircase was worn and there was a damp patch on the wall. No doubt this was the best they could afford, but her heart ached when she thought of the comfort in which Garnet had been reared. She mounted to the upper storey and rang the bell. From within came the sounds of movement and then, slowly, the door opened.

'Did you forget something?' Nicholas began and stopped, his hand still on the knob, his mouth open. Contrary to her expectations he was shaved and dressed and the room behind him was neat enough.

'Good morning, Mr Brocklehurst.' She took advantage of his hesitation to step past him.

'Mrs Webber.' He pronounced her name automatically, dully.

'You had best close the door,' she advised. 'I'm sure you would wish our talk to be private.'

'Garnet went out.' He took her advice, still looking bemused.

'I saw her crossing the street. She did not, of course, see me. My business is with you.'

'I don't think you and I have much to say to each other,' he demurred.

'You're quite correct and therefore we need not detain each other long,' she said, smiling tightly. 'I understand that you intend to—wed my daughter.'

'Tomorrow, at Marylebone Parish Church.' He gave her a defiant look and added, 'I have the ring and the licence.'

She had not come a moment too soon. Concealing relief, she enquired,

'And how much pecuniary advantage do you gain from the alliance?'

'I am deeply attached to your daughter,' he started to say, but she cut him short ruthlessly.

'Pray let us have no cant about feelings of affection. I know that Garnet has made the acquaintance of Miss Ashton.'

'I could not have afforded to marry her before.' His tone was darkly sulky. 'Miss Ashton has been most generous.'

'To the tune of how much?'

'I scarcely think—' he began, and was interrupted crisply.

'Quite right, Mr Brocklehurst. You scarcely ever do think. How much?'

'Three thousand pounds.'

'A handsome wedding gift. Is she to attend the ceremony?'

He shook his head.

'I understand Miss Ashton is confined to her room with a slight chill this week.'

So Victoria was rendered temporarily impotent. The gods, Fanny thought, with unwonted classicism, smile on me.

'And the—remuneration?' she enquired delicately.

'Miss Ashton is to bestow a dowry upon Garnet after the ceremony.'

'You have written confirmation of that?'

'Garnet has Miss Ashton's word,' he answered.

Which was probably sufficient. The Ashtons were honourable.

'I wonder if you can recall the last time we met?' Fanny mused.

'I'm not likely to forget it,' he retorted. 'You came to the theatre at York and tried to buy me off.'

'I seem to recall that you accepted the money,' Fanny reminded him. 'Five hundred sovereigns for which you signed a receipt. Your price seems to be rising, Mr

Brocklehurst.'

'I am not being bought off this time,' he said.

'Oh, I think you will be.' She gave him a slow curving smile. 'My daughter is to receive the money this time and you may find the task of charming it out of her rather more difficult than you anticipate.'

'Garnet happens to be in love with me.'

'She also happens to have lived with you these past two years. I've no doubt she knows you a trifle better than she did.'

'What is it you want?' he muttered uneasily.

'It is more a question of what you want.' Her voice was smooth silk. 'You don't truly wish to saddle yourself with a wife, do you? You are not, I venture to say, a marrying man. And there is your career, your unrecognised talent. It would take years for you to establish yourself in London and, by then, you would, I fear, be a somewhat elderly Romeo. If you were to try your luck in New York, however, I believe that English actors are greatly in demand there.'

'Whenever we meet,' he said, not without humour, 'you are always mightily concerned to send me elsewhere.'

'I have a ticket here.' She withdrew it from her purse and laid it on the table. 'The ship sails at midnight. At what hour does Garnet return?'

'At around four.'

'Then I would advise you to be gone by three. Pack your things and leave her the customary note of regrets. I will not, of course, have my name brought into this affair and you will not reveal your destination.'

'You seriously believe that I will go to New York!'

'When you reach the States,' she continued, as if he had not spoken, 'I want you to go to this address.' She laid a slip of printed cardboard next to the ticket. 'The gentleman there acts as my business agent over there. He also has connections with the theatre there and can give you some fruitful introductions. He will also have ready the sum of two thousand dollars to be handed to you when he is convinced that you arrived alone and unmarried.'

It was odd, but the longer she talked to Nicholas Brocklehurst the more he reminded her of her first husband, of Matthew Lawley who had betrayed her with her own sister. He had the same gypsyish good looks but there was a slackness about his jaw. Matthew had been strong, unswerving from his purpose. Fanny had a sudden, completely illogical desire to hear him tell her to go to hell, to keep her bribes because he loved Garnet and intended to make an honest woman of her.

'What guarantee do I have that you'll keep your word?' he asked.

'My word must suffice.' Disappointment

made her voice harsh. 'However, you do have my guarantee that if you attempt to marry my daughter you will never again set foot on an English stage. I am not without influence.'

'Then I'll write the note.'

He had given in so easily that she was ashamed for him, and more ashamed on Garnet's behalf that her daughter should have lost her head over such a man.

'Tell her that you are already married,' she said, 'and cannot therefore go through with what would be a bigamous ceremony.'

'I am very fond of her.' There was a futile belligerence in his tone.

'But you don't allow it to interfere with your common sense.' She nodded at him briskly and moved to the door. 'In that you display commendably sound judgment. Good-day to you, sir, and goodbye.'

She had opened and closed the door before he could offer any help. At the foot of the stairs she paused for a moment to draw a deep breath and control the trembling of her legs. The interview, straightforward as it had been, had taken more out of her than she anticipated.

She had memorised the Ashton address, but she had no desire to call upon Victoria. Instead, acting upon her own shrewd analysis of the life Sir Henry would be leading in London, she hailed a cab and had herself driven to White's Club.

No female was, of course, admitted within its hallowed portals but the imposing major-domo agreed to take in her note. He would see, he added grandly, if Sir Henry were at liberty.

Only a few minutes elapsed before, glancing through the window of the cab, she saw Sir Henry emerging between the marble columns.

'Fanny, what in the world brings you to London?' He had reached the side of the cab and was opening the door.

'Private business. Have you leisure to talk? I would not presume but it is important.'

'Have you had lunch?' he asked.

'Not yet. I am anxious to speak to you privately, Henry.' She laid a faint emphasis on the adverb.

'I know a discreet restaurant where we may talk undisturbed. It is not bad news, I hope?'

'They are all well at home,' she assured him.

He gave a brisk order to the cabbie and climbed up into its interior, settling himself opposite her with a slight grunt.

'You look very well,' Fanny said truthfully. 'The last time we met you had your foot on a stool!'

'I still suffer the occasional twinge of gout,' he admitted. 'I put it down to the damp Northern winters. Certainly it was not caused by over-indulgence. I was always an abstemious man.'

'Indeed you were.' She gave him a cool little

smile.

'I was sorry to read about Pearl and Larch.' He gave her a glance of embarrassed sympathy. 'A sad tragedy.'

'Yes.' A shadow of pain flitted across her face before she bowed her head.

'This is the restaurant. I think you will find the food to your taste.'

He paid the cab fare and escorted her into the pine-panelled foyer. Despite the independence she had always cultivated it was pleasant to be with a male escort. Fanny enjoyed the small attentions of the waiter as her chair was pulled out, her napkin unfurled. It was agreeable to leave the choice of menu to Henry and to have the wine waiter hover, anxious that the vintage be approved.

'So what brings you to London?' he enquired at length.

'I had business in the city. Mill business.'

'You're still managing the mill?'

'On behalf of Esther's son. He has settled to it very well, though his coming was a shock to me. We never dreamed that Esther and Philip ever had a child.'

'And to keep the fact of his existence a secret! I find that incredible.'

'Esther has never been quite like other people,' she reminded him. 'One cannot judge her by precisely the same standards.'

'I suppose not.' He gave her a pitying look, thinking it a damned shame that such a fine woman should be cursed by such relatives.

'I thought that I would call upon Garnet.' She toyed with a bit of lobster, aware that he had flushed slightly. 'Oh, I know it is a weakness in me to want reconciliation, but she is still my daughter for all the scandal she has caused me.'

'I cannot help feeling that Miss Garnet has been more sinned against than sinning,' he pronounced.

'Oh, but you are right. She was no more than a child, an inexperienced girl and he a practised seducer! I blame myself for not having realised the danger!'

'Did you see her?' he enquired.

'She had gone out,' Fanny said. 'I had an interview, a most unpleasant interview with Nicholas Brocklehurst. I told him quite frankly that it was time they wed, and he told me that a wedding had been arranged.'

'I didn't know that!' There was dismay in his ejaculation.

'He has persuaded her to agree to a secret ceremony at Marylebone Parish Church tomorrow,' Fanny said. 'I must confess that I was relieved, though he was not the husband I would have chosen for her, but something in his manner made me question him more closely and at last he admitted the truth.'

A solitary tear glittered on her lashes and coursed slowly down her cheek.

'My dear Fanny, there is no need to distress

yourself,' Sir Henry said, startled at this evidence of weakness in one whom he had always considered strong.

'Nicholas Brocklehurst doesn't intend to marry her at all,' Fanny said with a sob. 'He will leave her waiting at the church, and she will not be able to endure the shame of it! It seems that he has a wife already.'

'Surely not!'

'He showed me his marriage licence.' She dabbed at her eyes. 'Some small part actress whom he deserted years ago! I could not believe that any man could be so perfidious! He was without regrets or conscience as he told me.'

'Miss Garnet will need a mother's concern now,' Sir Henry said.

'Alas! if only that were so.' She heaved a quivering sigh. 'The truth is that my sudden appearance on the scene will only make Garnet suspect that I had some hand in the business. She will set her face ever more firmly against my authority.'

'It will be a very great shock to her,' he agreed.

'So great that I fear she might be driven to do something desperate. Oh, Henry, you are the one person I know in London, the only one I could think of from whom to seek help. Our families may have been estranged, but I still like to imagine that we are friends.'

'There is no imagination in it at all,' he

declared. 'I have always had the greatest regard for you, Fanny.'

'It is of Garnet that I am thinking,' she said. 'To have her whole life ruined by one thoughtless action and that taken through innocence! She will never find a husband now, for gentlemen will forget that she has a great sweetness of nature and remember only that she was ruined by a scoundrel!'

'Would you like me to visit her?'

'Would you, Henry?' She bestowed on him a somewhat shaky smile. 'I didn't dare to suggest it, but you have the experience to deal with such situations—and Garnet would listen to your advice.'

'I shall give what help I can,' he allowed.

'It is not financial assistance of which she stands in need,' Fanny said earnestly. 'I am not without means, though I fear she would be too proud to accept anything from me. What she needs is to be valued, cherished as a young lady should be cherished. If her father had only lived—but there, he was elderly and his health was poor. Would you really go and see her? Will not Victoria object?'

'Why should she?' he asked in surprise.

'Oh, some daughters might,' she said vaguely. 'You are an attractive man, Henry, much improved in health since you came south! Victoria might fear the loss of her own influence over you.'

'Victoria is my daughter, not my keeper,' he

returned, somewhat testily. 'She is confined to the house with a chill anyway.'

'The contrast between her position and Garnet's is acutely painful to me,' Fanny murmured.

'Will you leave the matter in my hands and trust me to deal with it?' he asked abruptly. 'Allow me to demonstrate that our old comradeship is not a mere pious memory for me.'

'It would be the most tremendous weight off my mind,' she confessed.

'Then leave it with me.' He all but patted her hand.

'You're very gallant, Henry.' She essayed another diffident smile. 'One misses that in the younger generation!'

CHAPTER SEVEN

Garnet sat as motionless as stone. She felt as she imagined a stone might feel were it sentient; heavy, gross and dull. So dull that it was an effort to string two coherent thoughts together. She gazed at the letter. It lay on the table where she had thrown it after the third or fourth reading. If she read it a hundred more times it would make no more sense than it had after the first reading, but its phrases beat in her brain.

'Dearest Garnet,

I'm truly sorry to spring this upon you without warning, but the fact is that I can't go through with the wedding. It isn't that I'm not fond of you. I've always told you that you're a stunner. The truth is that I already have a wife and the law won't allow a fellow to have two. I got married years ago and we've not lived together for most of them, but she's not about to grant me a divorce! It's clear to me that you're not a girl who'd be content with anything less than marriage, and it's also clear to me that you have a lot of talent and will likely go far in the profession. So. I'm off to try my luck elsewhere. Wish me good fortune and my thanks for everything you've meant to me,

Nicholas.'

The deliberately callous phrasing, the airy revelation that he already had a wife, the assumption that she would be as ready as he to shrug off two years of living together—these were beyond her understanding. She would never have dreamed of sending such a letter even to one whom she had ceased to love. Perhaps Nicholas had never really loved her at all. From the beginning it had been she who had pursued him, and the knowledge of that made her cheeks burn. It had been she who had first admired him when he had played Orlando and Mercutio at the theatre in York. Even when she had discovered that her mother had bribed him to leave the district she had

104

followed him, at first with some vague notion of getting her own back, but when he had greeted her with every appearance of delight her intention, never very clear, had faltered, and she had convinced herself that in time they would marry. Her teeth clenched on the word 'fool', and then she was dull and motionless once more.

There were footsteps on the staircase, a ringing of the doorbell. Her first glad surmise that it was all a heartless prank and that Nicholas had returned died into ashes at once. The letter was too flippantly cruel for any return to be contemplated. She rose, moving on leaden feet across the room, and opened the door.

'Miss Garnet, may I come in?' Sir Henry asked.

For a moment she stared at him without recognising him. She had never invited him to visit the apartment, feeling instinctively that against such a background she would scarcely appear to advantage. Then the remaining colour fled from her cheeks and she heard herself say faintly,

'Please. Do come in by all means.'

By a sad irony the apartment was neater than it had been for months. Nicholas had taken everything that was his, had even made the bed and washed the cups. There was nothing save the letter to prove that he had ever existed at all.

'I apologise for intruding,' Sir Henry was saying.

'I beg your pardon?' Garnet stared at him blankly.

'I said that I was sorry to intrude,' he repeated patiently. 'The truth is that I find myself in the neighbourhood and so took the liberty of calling.'

In his own ears the excuse sounded lame enough, but a glance at the girl's face made him realise that she was in a state of shock where anything he said might have been accepted without question. The open letter on the table and her twitching hands hinted at the truth of what Fanny had told him. He felt and controlled within himself a ferocious indignation that a young woman of gentle breeding should be treated thus.

'There is no rehearsal tonight, is there?' She was clearly making a tremendous effort to pull herself together and behave normally.

'Not as far as I know. I leave the organisation of the company to the Ryans. I merely called in the hope that you might be induced to take supper with me this evening.' Hesitating, he added, 'You and your young— er—gentleman, of course. One doesn't wish to intrude.'

'It's no intrusion.' She spoke sharply, her eyes suddenly dry and burning.

'But I am intruding? Perhaps I come at an inopportune moment?' He paused again, regarding her.

'I am—the truth is that I have had something of a shock.' She was too heartsick to dissimulate any longer. 'My—Mr Brocklehurst has left me rather abruptly and I am—will not be seeing him again.'

'I am sorry to hear it.' Sir Henry gave her a sympathetic look. 'I assumed that you and the young gentleman had planned—but there! it is none of my business.'

'Mr Brocklehurst and I had talked of marriage,' Garnet said, in a dry, harsh little voice. 'That is over now, so there is nothing to prevent me from accepting your invitation.'

'I wish,' Sir Henry said with a fervency that belied his years, 'that I were a younger man. In my day the horsewhip was occasionally employed to excellent effect.'

'On horses it might prove efficacious,' Garnet said with a faint smile, 'but I doubt if it would prove useful with actors.'

'And a young man who cannot appreciate the best when it is laid before him deserves only the worst,' he said heartily.

'As you say.' She turned away to hide her trembling lip, picking up the letter and folding it over and over.

'My dear Garnet, if I may call you so,' he said with an earnestness that surprised even himself, 'allow me to express not merely my sympathy that your plans should be spoiled, but the undeniable pleasure I cannot help feeling that no bar to our increased friendship now exists.'

But he didn't mean friendship. Garnet's numb feeling of shock was giving way to a further surprise, in its elements as unwelcome as the first. Sir Henry, she thought, was old! He could be her grandfather, had he married in his youth. The jests with which she had greeted his attentions were soured in her memory now that there was nobody with whom to share them. For a moment she was tempted to cry out in revulsion that he was too old, too spent even to act as an escort, and then something harder and more calculating, something that Fanny would have recognised and approved, broke through. Sir Henry, for all that he was elderly, was still attractive and he was wealthy, so wealthy that he could buy anything he pleased.

'I am already in debt to you for your kindness to me,' she said slowly.

'My dear young lady!' He possessed himself of her hand and patted it. 'You must not give that a thought. I am assured that the Ryans look most favourably upon your work.'

'It is only work.' The new, harder Garnet sighed. 'The theatre should be a vocation but, for me, it is merely a way of earning a living.'

'You could go home,' he suggested.

'To Sabre Hall?' Her upward glance was swift and forbidding. 'There have been too many scandals in our family already, Sir

Henry. My mother would never permit me to go home unless I were respectably married.'

'There is then no possibility—?' He hesitated.

'None.' Saying it was like closing a door. She took a long breath and continued steadily, 'Mr Brocklehurst was already married. I learned of it only today.'

Sir Henry wisely refrained from sympathy. Instead he said, after a discreet pause,

'If you have no rehearsal tonight I trust you will favour me with your company at supper. The truth is that I am somewhat at a loss with Victoria indisposed with a chill. She has been my companion for so long that when she is not well—it would be a great kindness on your part.'

'That's very good of you. I shall put on my hat.' She looked round vaguely, saw it on its hook, and went over to take it. Her fingers felt numb and clumsy.

'I shall wait for you below.' Sir Henry gave her a faint but reassuring smile and went out again.

A queer sense of unreality had stolen over her. She tied the ribbons on her hat and pinched colour into her white cheeks. The girl who had read the letter seemed to have changed into a different person with neither heart nor feelings. Her eyes were as cool as if they had never gazed on Nicholas's dark beauty and there was a new, grim set to her lips. Too grim perhaps? She consciously relaxed the muscles of her mouth and showed her white teeth in a small, demure smile, feeling nothing but surprise that the girl who was reflected in the mirror looked as if nothing inside her had changed at all.

Sir Henry was elderly but he was rich and a widower. At least it would be pleasant to be escorted by a personable man. Anything was better than staying here amid the ruins of all her dreams and hopes to brood on the memories of might-have-been.

He was waiting to help her into his carriage and she was struck by the contrast between his attentiveness and the casual indifference with which Nicholas had begun to treat her.

'This is a real pleasure for me.' He was smiling at her. 'There are times when Victoria, fond of her as I am, begins to—well, let us say that a daughter should have her own circle of friends. Victoria devotes herself to me and, in consequence, her own social life diminishes. Perhaps, had there been more children, but my wife, Elizabeth, died when Victoria was a girl. She'd ailed since her birth.'

'And you did not remarry?' Garnet was not much interested in Sir Henry's life, but tried to display polite attention.

'First there was Victoria, and then my own health wasn't good. I am inclined to think that our bodies are affected by our minds for, since I left Yorkshire with its sad associations, my gout comes far less frequently.'

If that held true for everybody, she thought dully, then at that moment she would be seriously ill, when in fact she felt perfectly healthy. Only her heart had turned into a leaden weight.

'It might be the climate. It can be very damp.'

As she spoke an unexpected longing for the cool wind that ruffled her hair when she rode across the moors sprang up in her mind. It was a long time since she had been on horseback. She had often ridden with Larch in the past, he tall and lean in the saddle, herself laughing as they raced through the heather. She had enjoyed a warm friendship with her cousin, unaffected by any stirring of sexual desire, and word of his and her sister's death had filled her with grief.

'But you miss it?'

They had reached the restaurant, and his coachman was holding open the door, so she didn't reply immediately but, when they were seated in a secluded alcove with smoked salmon before them, she said, in a voice from which she made no attempt to hide the wistfulness,

'Sometimes, after a hard day, I would do anything in the world to return to Yorkshire, but my mother would never permit it. I can't blame her. I must be a sad disappointment.'

'Fanny always had high standards,' he

nodded.

'I forget that you knew her when you were all young together,' Garnet said.

'Before our families quarrelled.' He nodded, memory in his face. 'My parents never forgave Philip for eloping with Esther. They disowned him and the Ashton property came to me. I didn't want it. I had my mind set on a career in the Church, but there were responsibilities I couldn't avoid. So I married Elizabeth and cut myself off from the Sabres, though I never ceased to have respect and friendship for Fanny. She had an unfortunate experience with her first marriage, and I was pleased that she found happiness in her second.'

'My father was a good man,' Garnet said softly.

'I would like to have met him.' Sir Henry gave her a kindly glance and added, 'You must not allow your own recent disappointment to spoil the rest of your life, my dear. You are still very young and it is the privilege of the young to make mistakes.'

'My mother would not allow me to enter Sabre Hall again,' Garnet heard herself saying, 'unless I were respectably married.'

'It's possible that you will be.' He sipped his wine, regarding her steadily across the table.

'But not to a young man.' The quiet vehemence in her tone surprised even herself. 'I am done with young men, Sir Henry.'

112

But they were not, perhaps, done with her. Sir Henry was faintly astonished to discover how much the idea displeased him.

'Garnet, may I call you so?' he said abruptly.

'Of course.'

'And you must call me Henry. There are few people who call me that these days.'

'Yes, of course,' Garnet said again mechanically. It seemed to her that she was destined to go on answering mechanically for the rest of her life.

'It is not perhaps the right moment in which to speak,' he was continuing, 'but I suspect that any moment might be difficult. The truth is that I have become increasingly fond of you during these past weeks. I am in many ways a lonely man. Money does not buy contentment or companionship.'

'Victoria—' she began.

'Victoria has always been a most dutiful and loving daughter, but there comes a time when a man begins to feel the need for a more intimate relationship. Not perhaps in the fullest sense unless it was your pleasure, but a union based upon affection and mutual consideration might prove of the greatest benefit.'

'Are you asking me,' Garnet said tensely, 'to be your mistress?'

Some such idea had been in his mind but, looking at her white face with the tendrils of brown hair curling round her brow, he found himself saying,

'My dear, I am asking you to be my wife.'

She had not expected that the question would be asked so soon and, for an instant as her eyes met his, panic swept through her. Charming and wealthy Sir Henry might be, but he was past sixty to her nineteen years, old enough to be her grandfather. The image of Nicholas flashed behind her eyes—beautiful, faithless Nicholas who had drained her of her capacity for loving, and left her an empty husk. The girl who had known how to love raised her chin in a gesture curiously reminiscent of Fanny and said coolly,

'I am grateful for the honour you have shown me, but perhaps if you are inspired by motives of pity—'

'I would not insult you by offering out of pity,' he interrupted warmly. 'If I don't seize my opportunity now you will likely be snatched up by some other man before I catch my breath.'

It seemed to her highly unlikely, but she allowed her lashes to flutter down while a faint smile played about her lips.

'My dear, we could be married as soon as you please,' Sir Henry said eagerly. 'By special licence, if you so wish! I would not seek to interfere with your theatrical career.'

'It means nothing to me,' she said. 'I told you that I have no vocation for the stage.'

'Perhaps you would like to visit Yorkshire?

In the summer time even I can endure the climate!'

'To return north?' For the first time a hint of a sparkle came into her grey eyes and she leaned forward slightly. 'Would you be willing to go north for a while?'

'There are times when I grow exceedingly weary of London,' Sir Henry said, patting her hand. 'It would be pleasant to go home, for the summer at least.'

It was none too subtle a bait, but the word 'home' struck a chord in her unresponsive heart. She heard herself saying,

'After we were married we could visit Yorkshire.'

'Your mother would receive you?'

'When I was respectably married, yes.' For a moment her pretty lips had a bitter twist. 'There has been too much scandal in the Sabre family and she will tolerate no more.'

If she returned to Sabre Hall it would be as Lady Ashton, rich and respectable, not as the erring daughter who had run away with a rascally actor. She would have money and position and somewhere, sometime, Nicholas might hear and regret—

'I beg your pardon?' She became aware that Sir Henry was speaking to her.

'I was saying that we could write to your family and invite them,' he repeated.

'No!' She spoke sharply, a frown rippling across her brow. 'I would prefer to be married as soon as possible, by special licence. There is nothing to prevent us, is there?'

'Nothing in the world.' A fleeting thought of Victoria's possible reaction crossed his mind, but he brushed it aside. 'We can be wed quietly in a few days and make our visit to Yorkshire a honeymoon trip.'

The word 'honeymoon' jarred on her. Honeymoons were taken by handsome young men and girls in love. Sir Henry was elderly and she herself would never again fall in love.

'That would be very pleasant,' she said at last. 'It would be nice to go back and see the family.'

'Pleasant' and 'nice' were words that matched the shade of her mood. For the rest of her life, she decided bleakly, she would never again feel passionately about anything.

'We should have ordered champagne.' He poured more of the wine for them both and raised his own glass. 'To you, my dear, and may I never give you cause to regret the decision you have made.'

She sipped her own wine, tasting it acid on her tongue. His voice, urbane and cultured, was continuing, talking of plans to be made, of the ring she would prefer.

'A diamond, of course. One can never go wrong with a good stone, and young ladies like diamonds, don't they?'

Diamonds, she thought, with no lifting of the heart, would be very suitable.

'I have been thinking,' Sir Henry said, 'that it might be more prudent to marry and then acquaint Victoria with the news. She is abed with a chill and the preparations and the actual ceremony might prove too much of a strain.'

He was evading her gaze. Clearly word of his intending marriage would upset Victoria. Garnet didn't particularly care. Victoria Ashton had already made her disdain for the Sabres abundantly clear. People who had a little money always thought they could do anything, could shape and twist people's lives to their own design. Well, in future, she would be the one to do the shaping.

'You will write to your family then?' Sir Henry was enquiring.

'Yes, of course.' Answering, she was struck by a sudden thought. 'It's dwindled since I left Yorkshire! Grandmother Fausty is gone and Pearl and Larch. I know that Cousin Sabre is there now but I never met him and I can't think of him as family.'

'My brother's son.' Sir Henry looked thoughtful. 'I too find it difficult to realise that Philip and Esther actually had a son. If they had not then Sabre Hall would have gone to your Aunt Gobnait.'

'She wouldn't have wanted it. She always like the farm at Batley Tor much better.'

'No, it was your mother who always loved Sabre Hall,' Sir Henry reflected. 'When we were all youngsters together she was the one

117

who helped with the mill accounts. Patrick never could be bothered with the business side of things.'

He sounded as if he had been a little in love with her mother. There was a wry irony in the thought that under different circumstances he might have been her father. Now, without quite knowing how it happened, she found herself engaged to him.

'I won't keep you out late tonight. A bride requires her beauty sleep.'

His voice was gently teasing and there was something in the look he gave her that held the promise of a fire long dead being rekindled. Presumably the marriage would not be one in name only then. The prospect neither excited nor disgusted her.

'If you will excuse me.' She rose, making a vague gesture in the direction of the cloakroom.

There were no other ladies titivating before the mirror. Garnet stood for a few moments, hands resting on the narrow shelf, contemplating her own image. In feature she was too much like her Aunt Gobnait to be pretty, but she had fine eyes and a skin not yet marred by greasepaint. As Lady Ashton she would look distinguished.

The letter, folded small, was in her reticule. She took it out, smoothed it flat and, without reading it again, began to tear it into minute strips. There was no emotion in her at all.

CHAPTER EIGHT

'We get along very well together, don't we?' Sabre remarked, reining in his horse and turning to smile at Rose.

'I like to think so.' She returned his smile with one of her own in which there was a hint of coquetry.

She had never known before what a delightful pastime flirtation could be. Pearl had been the one who had known how to coax and cajole, lowering her lashes, shaking her fair curls over her pink cheeks. Garnet had been more interested in horses until the night they had all gone to the theatre in York and she had seen Nicholas Brocklehurst.

'Something wrong?' Sabre watched the fading of her smile.

'I was wondering if Mother went to see Garnet while she was in London,' Rose said.

'She didn't mention it?'

'Not to me, but then she wouldn't confide in me anyway.' Rose spoke without self-pity.

'I doubt if she did go,' Sabre said thoughtfully. 'Aunt Fanny has struck me from the beginning as a woman who knows her own mind and won't yield on a principle.'

'She never mentions Garnet now.' Rose tried to recapture her earlier mood but her lower lip trembled slightly.

'Perhaps the actor fellow will marry her.'

'I think, if that had been in his mind, it would have happened by now,' Rose said.

'Your sister must love him very much to endure such circumstances,' Sabre said.

'Yes.' Rose heaved a brief sigh.

'You would never do such a thing?' He was still looking at her.

'Oh, I don't know.' The ready colour flamed into her face and then she raised her head, her blue eyes steady on his face. 'If I loved a man,' she said slowly, 'then I would follow him and stay with him no matter what the circumstances might be.'

'Defying convention?'

'If necessary.' Her cheeks were scarlet now but her glance remained unwavering.

'A man who loved a girl would not ask such a sacrifice,' he returned. 'I would not ask it of you.'

'Oh?' There was the lilt of surprise in her voice.

'Rose, it is time I married.' He spoke abruptly, his hand tightening on the reins he held. 'I am thirty-seven years old and I have the responsibilities of the mill and the estate. A man needs a wife, but I have waited until now because it's only now that I have met someone with whom I feel I can spend the rest of my life.'

'With me?'

'With you, Cousin Rose.' He leaned to tap

her cheek gently with his forefinger. 'I'm twice your age and you may not have considered me as a romantic figure, but I would be a good husband. Now what do you say?'

'I think you should speak to my mother,' Rose said faintly.

She had imagined how it might be if Sabre ever proposed marriage to her. She had pictured herself swinging lazily in a hammock though there wasn't such a thing at Sabre Hall, and he would have told her that her eyes were stars he could no longer resist, and there would have been a moon rising. The entire scene had been as unreal as the possibility that he actually would propose. And now here she sat, in her old riding habit with the patch on the elbow and the breeze tangling her hair, and he was businesslike and unemotional as if he were concluding a deal for wool or horses.

'I think your mother will be only too happy to give her permission,' Sabre said, a faint dryness creeping into his tone. 'I am more anxious to know your feelings on the matter.'

She longed to cry out that she was so deep in love that she would have followed him even had her mother objected, but her new-found confidence was not yet very strong and she answered instead, stammering a little,

'You must allow me a little time. I am—I would like to be married to you, but this is the first time you have spoken of it.'

'Didn't you have an inkling of what was in

my mind?' he enquired curiously.

'Not really. I have not,' she explained primly, 'been acquainted with many gentlemen.'

He threw back his head and gave a shout of laughter that set his horse dancing nervously.

'Rose, you're a tonic! A veritable tonic,' he exclaimed. 'Thank the Lord that Aunt Fanny had the sense to bring you to Sabre Hall when your father died! Had she taken you somewhere else some man would have swept you up before I'd a chance to meet you.'

It was flattering to be told that though she doubted if it were true. The few gentlemen she had met had always wanted to gaze admiringly at Pearl, talk to Garnet and, whatever attention they had left over, was generally employed in a pat on the head and a kindly word for the youngest sister.

'I'll talk to your mother as soon as we get home.' He reached again to touch her cheek.

'You ride ahead. I'll follow.' She wanted suddenly to be alone, to savour the possibilities that lay ahead.

'Ride carefully.' He nodded at her, gathered up the reins and galloped away.

She watched him go, wishing that she had found something romantic to say that would have expressed her feelings, instead of blushing and stuttering like a schoolgirl. But at least he had asked her and the reality of that was more exciting than any dream she had dreamed. And it was good now to be alone for a while, to walk her mare slowly over the turf, to feel the wind cooling the nape of her neck on this afternoon of brilliant summer.

'Rose! Hey, Rose!'

Her drifting attention was caught by the voice hailing her from further up the slope.

'Aunt Gobnait!' There was genuine pleasure in Rose's voice. The one person she didn't mind seeing at that moment was her aunt.

'I saw you from the top of the hill,' Gobnait declared, cantering towards her. 'Why did Sabre ride off in such a great hurry? Did he see me coming or are you both at outs?'

'Neither. He went on ahead, that's all. There's nothing wrong is there?'

'A letter from Garnet. I've been staring at it for an hour, trying to believe my eyes. You'd better look for yourself and tell me if you get the same sense out of it that I did.'

She fumbled in the pocket of her breeches, drew out a folded slip of notepaper and passed it to the younger girl as she dismounted.

Rose, unfolding it and scanning the few lines it contained, raised her head, her eyes huge.

'It says that Garnet is married,' she said blankly. 'She's married Sir Henry Ashton!'

'That was what I thought it said.' There was a rueful twist to Gobnait's lips.

'But surely she was living with Nicholas Brocklehurst,' Rose said.

'Now she is apparently living with Henry, as his wife.'

'She says.' Rose referred again to the letter. 'She says, "I have known Sir Henry for some time and the affection between us has become mutual. We are planning to return to Yorkshire when he has sorted out his affairs here. He has told his daughter and she was kind enough to wish us happiness. I hope very much that you will wish us the same. I am writing to Mother at the same time and trust that she will be pleased".'

'Oh, Fanny will be delighted,' Gobnait said. 'She never wanted Garnet to marry the actor.'

'Garnet doesn't mention him at all. What do you think can possibly have happened?'

'Who knows?' Gobnait shrugged. 'Lord, but this is one turn of events I never expected! Henry and Garnet. My niece and my late husband's brother-in-law.'

'I'd forgotten that.'

'Oh, the Ashtons and the Sabres have always been entangled,' Gobnait said. 'Esther eloped with Philip and Henry married Elizabeth Grant.'

'And you married Edward Grant.'

'In middle age, when everyone thought that I was past the age of marrying.' Gobnait laughed. 'I broke all the rules, you know. I lived in happy sin for years, bore a daughter, and when Matthew died, instead of doing penance by devoting myself to good works for the rest of my life, I married Edward and went off to Africa. We were happy together too, in a comfortable, middle-aged way. Now it looks as if Garnet is following in my footsteps. So the pattern is repeated.'

'He's old though, isn't he?' Rose said. 'And Garnet is young.'

'Whereas Edward and I were both middle-aged? No doubt Garnet has her reasons.'

'And they're coming here in a couple of months. Do you think they'll stay at Sabre Hall? Will Mother allow it?'

'Who knows?' Gobnait shrugged again.

'They used to live at Ashton House, didn't they? Victoria Ashton and her father,' Rose queried.

'It was the grandest house in the district.' There were memories in Gobnait's green eyes. 'We used to visit there sometimes when we were girls. Sir John and Lady Ashton were still alive then, of course. He was a nice man, quiet and courteous. *She* was a holy terror! Always wore immense turbans, and all her jewellery at once! I suppose it went to Victoria. Heavens, but she must be in her mid-thirties now. Garnet has a step-daughter older than she is!'

'She says that Victoria wished them happiness,' Rose said.

'Which means that she was not actually present at the ceremony. If you ask me,' Gobnait said, with an unexpectedly youthful giggle, 'Henry has suddenly kicked up his heels and flung his cap over the windmill to prove there's life in him yet! I'd never have believed it!'

'What in the world will Mother say?'

'Ten to one that she'll be delighted! Fanny always enjoyed the whiff of a title. There's never been one in the Sabre family yet. Did you ever hear how my own father came to be given his name?'

'Grandfather Earl?'

'*His* father always expected to get a title and when one wasn't forthcoming, he named his son Earl anyway. I expect quite a lot of people thought that it *was* a title. Oh, we're a snobbish lot!'

'Lady Ashton,' Rose said thoughtfully, as if she were trying the name for size. 'It does sound rather grand.'

'As long as she is happy.' Gobnait pushed back her hat and frowned slightly. 'I always thought Henry rather a dull dog. Perhaps Garnet will liven him up a bit.'

'I had better start for home.' Rose moved with her awkward gait to remount.

'I'll come with you. I want to see Fanny's reaction. She'll have received her own letter by now,' Gobnait declared, following suit.

'It probably came while Sabre and I were out riding.' Rose stopped abruptly, realising that in her excitement over the revelation of her sister's tidings she had forgotten her own news.

'You and Sabre—' Her aunt, who picked up thoughts with a sensitivity of which few would have deemed her capable, paused.

'He has asked me to be his wife.' Safely in the saddle Rose gathered up the reins and blushed furiously.

'My dear, I couldn't be more pleased! It's an inevitable match really, isn't it?' Gobnait exclaimed.

'Inevitable?'

'Well, Esther did fool everybody by suddenly revealing that she and Philip had had a son who came along to inherit the property and knock everybody out of the running,' Gobnait said cheerfully. 'Oh, I know he's good-humoured and was happy to let everybody stay on, but if he'd taken a wife from outside the family she might have objected to a gaggle of female relatives. As it is you and Sabre will settle happily together, and Fanny will be as pleased about that as I'm wagering she is about Garnet's marriage to Henry! Sabre's a good man, Rose, and he'll be a better husband for having sown his wild oats first.'

'I have not actually accepted him yet,' Rose began.

'But you will.' Gobnait slapped her mount lightly on the rump as they broke into a trot. 'You'd be a fool to turn him down and I never took you for a fool!'

It was strange, but her approving remarks

dampened Rose's spirits slightly. It was, after all, a most suitable match, but the most suitable matches were not always the most romantic and something in the girl yearned for romance, for a taste of something thrilling and forbidden.

Esther came fluttering out of the house, scarves and shawl trailing and her pale hair escaping, as usual, from its pins, as they reached the front door. As usual too her conversation was a softly breathless monologue, interspersed with the irrelevancies which led many who knew her only slightly to regard her as moon-mazed.

'Two weddings in the family, though we did not, of course, get to go to dear Garnet's. She and Henry—and I was under the impression that he was a martyr to the gout! Have you received a letter from her too, Gobnait? Fanny is as pleased as if she set it up herself. They will stay here when they come, of course. She is writing to tell them so at once. If they do decide to settle then it may be possible for them to buy back Ashton House. And Sabre and you, Rose! I have hoped for so long that he would do the right thing!'

'I had a letter from Garnet, telling me that she has married Henry.' Gobnait swung herself to the ground and kissed her younger sister lightly on the cheek. 'I've no doubt that Fanny is pleased. Rose told me that Sabre has offered for her. It meets with your approval then?'

'I couldn't express to you how much,' Esther cried fervently. 'You know I am only just becoming accustomed to being a mother and I dreaded having to be mother-in-law to a complete stranger had Sabre chosen to marry one. As it is I am already Rose's aunt and I have no doubt that it will be very easy to be her mother-in-law too!'

'You're a very nice aunt,' Rose spoke warmly, though the sinking feeling was still inside her.

'We'd better go in. Rose, will you take the horses round to the stables? Oldfield drove Maggie down to the village. We ran out of sugar. At least we didn't actually run out, but I tipped it into the salt by mistake and my scones tasted most peculiar.' Esther caught at the end of an errant scarf, tucked it into her waistband, and drew Gobnait within.

Rose, dismounting, led the horses round to the stableyard. It seemed then that her engagement to Sabre was approved, just as Garnet's marriage to Sir Henry Ashton was regarded as right and fitting.

The older generation, she thought suddenly, had all outraged convention and now they expected the younger generation to set it right by behaving with the utmost decorum. Rose, who had never outraged convention in her life, thought wistfully that it might have been pleasant to have had the opportunity.

'I'll see to the horses.' Sabre, emerging from

the barn, spoke with the cheerfulness of one who sees his destiny cast in pleasant places. Aunt Fanny, already in high good humour after learning of Garnet's wedding, had briskly approved his proposal.

'I'm delighted, my dear Sabre. Rose is very young of course, but my own second husband was several years my senior and our union was a very happy one. I would suggest that you set a date in early spring. The worst of the bad weather ought to be over by then and, of course, Garnet will be at home.'

'I shall try and make her happy,' he had returned.

'Of course you will. Rose is a most fortunate girl.' Fanny had bestowed upon him one of her sweetest smiles.

Rose, he thought now as he took the reins from her, was a darling. He was not certain exactly when he had begun to discover the fact. Perhaps it had had something to do with his own sensations of boredom and disgust when he rose and fumbled for payment after the occasional nights he spent in York with a whore. Perhaps it was simply that she was there, small and gallant in her lameness, with the April face across which her varying moods flitted like sunshine and shadow. That he had also begun to desire her startled him. Certainly it was not something he intended to reveal until after the ring was safely on her finger. In Sabre's experience, well-brought-up young

130

ladies shied like nervous horses when the subject of physical passion arose.

'I spoke to your mother,' he said, turning his head to smile at her. 'I told her that I was ready to settle down and take a wife and asked if she'd any objections to my marrying you.'

'Which she had not?'

'Which she had not,' he agreed. 'I think that spring would be an excellent time. The worst of the winter will be over and the early lambing past and your sister will be back and able to attend.'

'That's six months off,' Rose said.

'Well, you're going to need a trousseau and a cake, things like that,' he said vaguely. 'You're not likely to change your mind, are you?'

His tone was lightly teasing and the pat he gave her shoulder was almost brotherly. Beneath his palm her shoulder felt slight and vulnerable. In a moment he would be tempted to pick her up, carry her into the barn, and make the kind of violent love to her that would have sent her into a state of shock. He removed his hand hastily and said, in the same teasing tone:

'Or do you have a secret admirer tucked away in the village somewhere?'

'No, of course not.' Surprised and displeased, she answered him sharply.

'Then spring it is then!' He led the horses into the gloom of the stable, whistling under his breath.

Rose stared after him in disappointed bewilderment. He had patted her in exactly the same way as he patted his horse and he had not even attempted to kiss her. She had heard of husbands becoming unromantic after marriage, but it looked as if Sabre had no romantic feelings for her at all. She sighed, wishing that she were older and understood more, and turned back towards the house, pushing open the back door and entering the kitchen with much of her gaiety extinguished.

She had loved Sabre for a long time and yet, now that the promise of marriage had been given, she felt as if something vital were lacking. Perhaps reality was always smaller than expectation.

Her mother and the two aunts were in the drawing-room. She could hear Gobnait's voice raised in amusement.

'Well, Fanny, it looks as if two of your ambitions are about to be realised. Garnet is now wed into the aristocracy and Rose will be Sabre's wife.'

'You talk as if I were some kind of awful matchmaker,' Fanny reproved. 'Garnet has always made her own decisions. I'm only thankful that this time she seems to have made a sensible one. I'm pleased for Rose's sake that Sabre has made an offer. With her handicap she was unlikely to receive any others.'

'Why, Rose is a perfect darling!' That was

132

Aunt Esther's voice.

'I never said she wasn't.' Fanny's tone was slightly irritable. 'She's a dear, good girl for all that she always has her nose buried in a book, but the fact is that she's lame and most men would be put off by that. Fortunately Sabre is kind-hearted and he knows where his duty lies. After all, if he had never been born, Sabre Hall would have gone first to Gobnait and then to me and my girls. I think he has shown a very proper spirit in offering.'

Rose stayed to hear no more. Noiselessly she backed away and went into the study at the other side of the hall. This room with its crowded bookshelves and dark red hangings had become, by tacit consent, her own, private domain. She was the one in the family who read the most voraciously, the one who needed time in which to be alone. When she was alone she shaped her dreams in her mind.

Closing the door softly behind her she sat down in one of the leather armchairs, stretching her leg cautiously. It still ached if she stood on it for too long, and no matter how pretty the dress she wore she had only to raise the skirt an inch to see the ugly thick-soled boot. Sabre couldn't possibly be in love with her. Even Aunt Esther had spoken of her son's kind heart. To be married for kindness and pity struck her as the greatest humiliation anyone could suffer. She sat, her eyes closed and her teeth clenched against the pain that was sweeping through her, while in her mind the dream she had shaped crumbled and fell into nothingness. Sabre had asked her to be his wife because he knew it was expected of him, because he knew that nobody else was likely ever to ask her. A tear slid from beneath her lashes and splashed onto her hand.

'Rose, where in the world are you?' Fanny was calling in the hall.

If she went out now and told them what she knew they would smile at her and tell her not to be foolish. They might even persuade Sabre to talk to her and she couldn't endure the thought of his pretending love for her out of kindness. For the moment she too would have to pretend, until she had worked out some way of leaving Sabre Hall. For the first time she bitterly resented the lameness that kept her confined.

CHAPTER NINE

'Well, this is Dublin.' Gobnait gave her niece an amused look as they stood at the rail of the boat edging its way into harbour. 'The Lord knows what we're both doing here, but here we are!'

'I promised Grandmother Fausty that one day we'd go to Ireland together,' Rose repeated for the umpteenth time. 'I know she died before she could go, but I do feel obliged to keep my side of the promise.'

'As you've been telling us for weeks!' Gobnait put her arm round the other's shoulders and gave her a swift and affectionate hug. 'I never knew you had it in you to be so determined about anything!'

'I made a promise. After I'm married I won't be able to go rushing off all over the place,' Rose said lightly.

'You and Sabre could have made a honeymoon trip of it,' Gobnait said.

'Oh, it will be more amusing to explore with you,' Rose said. 'You know I can scarcely believe that we've arrived. I hadn't been on a trip since we came from New York.'

'By the time we get back to Yorkshire Garnet will probably have arrived,' Gobnait said. 'If I know Fanny she'll have spring-cleaned the entire house from top to bottom!'

'Then I'm glad I'm not there. Aunt, I believe we're landing!'

'So we are.' Gobnait craned her neck, standing on tiptoe to scan the crowds lining the wharf. 'I wonder if the uncles received my letter. We've not written to them since Mother died, and I'm not even certain they're still at the same place. They were always wanderers.'

'Will you recognise them after so long? How long is it since you saw them?'

'They came over with Cousin Cathy to spend a holiday in—the summer of thirty-nine.' Gobnait looked startled. 'Why, that's nearly half a century ago! It was the summer that Patrick was killed and Esther ran away with Philip Ashton. Then we found out that Cathy was expecting Patrick's child. That was an eventful summer!'

'The uncles will be older now,' Rose said.

'Forty years older. They were young boys then. We were all very young.' For a moment Gobnait's features had a wistful cast and then she waved her arm more vigorously, calling above the hooting of the tugs and the slap of rope as it uncoiled on the wharf. 'I see them! Stevie! Sean!'

Rose was quite certain that she could never have picked anyone out of the crowd at such distance and after such a time, but Gobnait, it seemed, had made no mistake. The two lean elderly men who looked as if they had been stamped from the same mould were waving back.

Somehow, amid the bustle of landing and the brief formalities of arrival, Rose found herself being heartily embraced and lifted up to a donkey trap while one of the uncles gave directions to a porter to follow with the luggage.

'We've booked rooms for you at the grandest guest house,' Sean—or was it Stevie?—was saying 'We've a cottage at the other side of town, but it's bachelor quarters and not fit to entertain ladies. Gobnait, you don't look a day older than when we saw you last.'

'And you've not learned yet to tell the truth,' Gobnait retorted.

'May God strike me down if I tell a lie,' he returned piously. 'You were a handsome girl and now you're a handsome woman, and one with a past too. There's wild Irish in you—or am I telling tales out of school before the child?'

'Not much point in trying to hide old scandals,' Gobnait said, 'and there have been plenty.'

'Aye, Fausty used to keep us in touch.' He climbed to the driving seat and gathered up the reins. 'We'll get you settled in and then we can talk to our heart's content! Tell me, is Sabre well and happy? We've a vested interest in that boy seeing as we were the only family he knew when he was growing up.'

'Esther thought it best to say nothing of his existence,' Gobnait said shortly.

'Well, she'd good reason, I dare say.' He shot a glance at Rose. 'It went against the grain not to be telling Fausty however that she'd a legitimate grandson, but she'd not have kept it to herself. Fausty never was good at keeping a secret, God rest her soul! The guest house is at the end of the Crescent. Two bedrooms and a sitting room for two weeks, and we'll be spending most of that time gossiping.'

'You mean that you two will be doing the

137

talking while Rose and I are condemned to listen,' Gobnait said wryly.

'There's precious few of the Sullivan family left to listen,' he retorted. 'To be thinking of it now! Only three of us left out of eight, and Mary in her convent is as good as dead. Here's the house. Sean's following on with the baggage.'

This then must be Stevie, the younger of Grandmother Fausty's twin brothers. She had always spoken of them both as a pair of scamps, settling to nothing, never marrying. It was hard to relate her description to the lean, grey-haired man who greeted them, but then he gave her a bright, mischievous look out of his dark eyes and she could see the boy still lurking in the elderly man.

The landlady, who boasted a patently false fringe and a clearly genuine bosom encased in black silk, shook hands, expressed surprise at their safe arrival from what she evidently regarded as foreign parts, and showed them into a suite of modest but comfortably furnished rooms.

'I've a casserole simmering and an apple pie with cream so fresh the cow hasn't missed it yet,' she informed them. 'Mr Sullivan, will you and your brother be staying on, for there's plenty to eat and you'll have plenty to say?'

Rose was glad rather than sorry when Stevie accepted for his brother and himself. Usually at the end of a journey she preferred to be

138

alone for a while to recoup her energies and adjust to her surroundings, but now she craved talk and distraction, anything to prevent her thoughts from running round and round and ending up always in the same place.

The suitcases were being carried up, the supper laid on the table, a fire lit against the evening chill, and Gobnait's clear, decisive tones blended with the softer accents of the Irish.

'Come and drink some tea.' The uncle called Sean tapped her on the arm. 'Glory be to God, but you're only a teeny bit of a thing! Pretty eyes though, eh, Stevie? It's no great wonder that Sabre admired them. And when is the wedding to be? We're counting on being invited, mark!'

She was spared the necessity of answering by Gobnait who, helping herself liberally from the steaming casserole, said cheerfully,

'In spring. Rose is scarce eighteen and doesn't need to rush. This trip is by way of being a last fling before she takes on the duties of a wife. But you've not heard the really astonishing news.'

'Fanny's getting wed again?' Stevie hazarded.

'Garnet has married Henry Ashton,' Gobnait told them.

'Philip's brother?'

'The very same.' Gobnait nodded her head.

'I thought she was off treading the boards

139

somewhere,' Sean said.

'She was, but now she has married Henry—Sir Henry, I should say. She wrote to tell us of it and apparently they are coming back to Yorkshire, though whether they will make a long or short stay I don't know.'

'He must be in his sixties!' Sean whistled under his breath and nudged his brother. 'What possessed the girl?'

'The Ashtons are rich, aren't they? Would that weigh with the girl?' Stevie enquired.

'Not with the Garnet I knew,' Gobnait said. 'But we've heard little of her since she left home. We shall have to find out when she comes.'

'Two weddings.' Sean whistled again. 'I take it that Fanny is pleased.'

'Very pleased.' Gobnait answered briefly.

'Ah, she's a great one, is Fanny!' Sean uncorked a bottle he had produced and poured a generous measure. 'I'll never forget how ashamed she was of her low, common, Irish relatives that summer we went over! She's a lady is Fanny.'

'She's not had an easy life,' Gobnait said.

'And you didn't make it easier by stealing away her first husband,' he continued.

'Matthew was no husband for Fanny. They were happier apart and he was happier with me,' Gobnait said tolerantly.

'And Fanny found herself a good second husband and had three girls.' Sean poured a second measure and lifted the tumbler. 'Pearl I never met, and Garnet I don't know yet, so here's to Rose who is the prettiest thing to land in Ireland these twenty years and will be making Sabre the finest wife in the world.'

'To Rose.' Gobnait raised her own glass and set it down again. 'Tell me your news now.'

'Where to begin?' Stevie laughed and leaned back in his chair. 'Sean and I make a living here and there from this and that! As I said there's only us and Mary left—Mother Prioress, that is! You knew that she was Superior of her convent now?'

'I heard. Of course, I've never met her,' Gobnait said.

'Well, she's not changed. When she was only a girl she behaved exactly as if she were a nun already,' Sean said. 'It's an awful pity, Rose, that you never knew the rest of us. Oh, we Sullivans never had much class, but we'd spunk! There was Fausty, going off to learn the reading and writing from an English lady who lived in the village, and then taking herself to England. She sent money home every year until she died, but she never came herself.'

'She was always talking of it,' Rose put in, 'but she died before she could come.'

'She'd have been proud of us. Fausty always thought the best of those she loved,' Stevie said.

'Bridie now was a good, hard worker,' Sean mused. 'Always kept us clean as any human

141

being could. She married late did Bridie. She and her man are gone now. Did you know her two children emigrated?'

'I thought they'd died,' Gobnait said.

'Perhaps they have by now. They went off to Australia—or South Africa. Somewhere like that.'

'Aunt Cathy died too, didn't she?' Gobnait said.

'Without ever speaking to any of us again. You see, Rose darling.' He turned to her. 'Our sister Cathy had a daughter, Catherine, whom she wanted to turn into a lady! Well, we went over to see Fausty and took Catherine with us to seek out a fine English lord and didn't the little minx get herself into trouble with your Uncle Patrick! Oh, he'd have married her quick enough if he'd lived.'

'He was killed by a drunken millhand, wasn't he?' Rose put in.

'Killed anyway.' Sean frowned and continued rather hastily. 'Then Catherine died when the child was born, and Cathy never spoke to any of us again. She and her man went in the Hunger. Peg too. Peg was the one with freckles. She used to get up at four o'clock in the morning and wash them in dew!'

'Where exactly is Aunt Mary's convent?' Rose enquired.

'Ten miles south of Dublin. You'll not be able to see her. It's a closed Order.'

'Surely for relatives there would be an

exception,' she said.

'Maybe so, but Mary's one of those people who won't even take what's due to them,' he shrugged. 'She'd refuse to see you and then chalk the sacrifice up as another jewel in her heavenly crown! Now be telling us about yourself, Rose darling. How long have you and Sabre been promised?'

'It's not official yet.' She spoke quickly, pain twisting inside her. 'I wanted to visit Ireland first, as Grandmother Fausty and I had planned to do.'

'And she wouldn't hear a single argument against it,' Gobnait said, pride in her voice. 'You'd never guess our quiet little Rose could be so determined. Sabre was all for making it a honeymoon trip, but she insisted that I come with her. Fanny would have come but she's too busy preparing for Garnet's arrival.'

'She'll be in favour again then?' Stevie asked the question idly.

'She's Lady Ashton,' Gobnait said, without emphasis.

'And what will you two be doing tomorrow?' Sean wanted to know. 'The old cabin's still standing by the way. That was where we were all born, Rose. We go over now and then to clean out the place.'

'We'll go and look at it,' Gobnait said, 'but not tomorrow.'

'Not shopping? You're not going to waste your first day in Dublin buying clothes and

143

geegaws!' he exclaimed.

'I was hoping there might be a Race Meeting,' Gobnait said. 'Mother used to tell me how, when she was a child, her dadda used to take her to the races.'

'And spend any money he won on a bottle of poteen and sweets for the rest of us,' Stevie grinned. 'Ah, he was a grand old man! There's a Meeting tomorrow and it'll be our pleasure to escort you two darling ladies.'

'One darling lady.' Rose smiled, twisting her hands together under the tablecloth. 'I really do begin to feel a little tired.'

'You need a good night's sleep and here we are, all talking you to death! In the morning you'll be fine. Sean, let's be making a move and then we can give these two the chance of a rest. One more drink and we'll be on our way,' Stevie declared.

'I thought I'd have a quiet day tomorrow,' Rose said, a little desperately. 'You know, sleep late, perhaps take a little walk, then make a list of people for whom I want to buy gifts. You go to the Race Meeting, Aunt.'

'I can't leave you by yourself on your first day in Ireland,' Gobnait objected.

'I shall be perfectly all right,' Rose assured her. 'You know you won't want to miss the Meeting.'

'It's the Ballyhine Cup,' Stevie said, 'and that's as nice a little race as you could hope to find.'

'You go,' Rose urged. 'I shall put my feet up, perhaps take a buggy ride.'

'That's settled then. We'll call for you around nine, Gobnait. Will you be laying a little wager on? Silver Lady is your best bet.'

'I'll make up my mind when I've seen her in the paddock,' Gobnait said.

The talk drifted to horses. Amidst it Rose made her goodnights and went to the smaller of the two bedrooms. Fanny had regarded it as an unjustifiable expense to book two sleeping chambers but had been overruled by Gobnait who had declared, 'I've slept alone for so long that I don't think I could endure a companion.'

Rose was glad she was to have the luxury of privacy. What she had resolved to do was so foreign to everything in her nature that she feared she would not be able to sustain her resolution in the face of her aunt's plans and projects for the wedding.

'You ought to wear blue, my love, not that I've any taste in fashion, and I hear a lot of brides are choosing white lace but I think with your eyes blue is your best shade. I don't suppose you'd think of having my Liza as attendant? I know she's only a servant but she's little and pretty, and she'd be thrilled to be asked.'

Gobnait had, to her niece's surprise, evinced a purely feminine interest in her forthcoming marriage. Even that had been easier to bear than Sabre's pleasant and affectionate conversation.

'When you come back from Ireland we'll go into York and I'll buy you a ring, a sapphire ring. Or would you like another stone?'

'A sapphire would be lovely,' she'd said primly.

'We'll be happy together, Rose. We suit well and this is one marriage of which the family approves. How do you think you will enjoy being mistress of Sabre Hall?'

He had spoken lightly and teasingly and she had looked at him in a kind of wonder, astonished that he shouldn't yet have realised that, no matter who owned Sabre Hall, her mother would always be the mistress there.

Fanny had been rather less amiable.

'This notion of rushing off to Ireland at the very moment your marriage is agreed and just before Garnet is expected home! If you want my opinion you've taken leave of your senses. You and Gobnait! But there's no sense in my trying to argue with you. You will go your own way as ever.'

It was fortunate that she had been too occupied with cleaning the house and deciding on the menus to offer more than a token resistance. Fortunate too that the trip was arranged so quickly there was no time for Fanny to think up new reasons why she ought not to go.

It had, in the end, been a relief to leave. Some part of her had longed, right to the end, for some word, some sign, that her cousin had proposed out of something more than kindness. If only he had put his arms round her and told her that he loved her too much to live without her, then she would have found grounds on which to build hopes for the future, but his occasional kisses had been lightly casual and he treated her still as if she were the young cousin for whom he felt no more than warm affection. To live as his wife, knowing she would never possess the deepest places in his heart, was a destiny not to be contemplated.

She looked now at her two locked and labelled trunks. There was no point in starting to unpack them. Her nightdresses and a change of undergarments were in a small carpet bag, and the rosary that had belonged to Grandmother Fausty was in her pocket. In her purse was the hundred sovereigns that she had drawn out of her allowance. Brides needed a dowry.

She was in bed, eyes closed and breathing even, when Gobnait put her head round the door some time later.

'The uncles are gone. Are you asleep?' She waited a moment, then apparently satisfied that her niece had dropped off, closed the door softly and retreated.

It was tempting to delay her decision, but Rose knew that the longer she put it off the harder it would be to leave. Yet she would have liked to visit some of the places of which her grandmother had spoken. Fanny had always been slightly ashamed of her lively, slightly eccentric mother but Rose had had a great affection for the old lady who had never lost her Irish brogue or her sense of fun. When she had been in the mood she had given vivid and racy accounts of her girlhood in the old country.

'We always had shoes for when we went to Mass. Always shoes, and a meal inside us. Dadda always saw to that, even when he'd taken a drop. He'd never have taken that if Mammy had lived, but she died when Sean and Stevie were born. They were the first twins born in the family, and then I went to England and had two sets of them! I wonder if there will be any more twins born in the future.'

'Not to me, Grandmother,' Rose thought now, and bit her lip to make a small pain to drive out a larger one.

Morning brought her aunt again, hat pinned securely to her top-knot of reddish grey hair, her skirt and jacket cut on elegant but mannish lines. She looked, Rose thought, as if she were hoping to be a competitor in the race, not a mere spectator.

'I'm just off. The landlady—her name is Mrs O'Byrne, by the way—has provided an enormous breakfast, so if you feel like getting up, there's a feast waiting—or shall I bring in something on a tray?' she enquired.

'I'll get up later.' Rose yawned.

'You do look a bit peaky, I must say.' Gobnait leaned over the pillow, anxiety shadowing her high-coloured countenance. 'Washed out! Are you certain you don't mind my going?'

'Go and enjoy yourself. The uncles are longing to show off their niece,' Rose said.

'I never have called them "uncle",' Gobnait said, effectively diverted. 'They're not much more than ten years older than I am, and they act younger most of the time! Well, if you're certain—'

'I shall have a lazy morning, eat some late breakfast, and probably go for a ride. Grandmother Fausty said it was easy to hire a buggy.'

'Nothing easier, I'm told. There are the uncles!' Gobnait waved through the window and blew a kiss to Rose. 'I'll see you later on then. I may lay a little wager on Silver Lady. Shall I put something on for you?'

'If you like.'

'Lord, but wouldn't Fanny disapprove!' Gobnait exclaimed, with one of her irrepressible giggles. 'You lazing in bed until noon and me running off to lose money at a race meeting.'

'Perhaps you'll win.' Rose yawned again, wishing the other would go.

'Perhaps I will. I begin to think this might be my lucky day,' Gobnait said, blowing another kiss as she strode through the door.

Rose sagged against the pillows, the moisture of relief springing on her palms and brow. If her aunt had delayed a moment longer her resolution would have faltered and she would have cried out her plans.

Now there was nothing to prevent her leaving; nothing save her own nervousness at taking what she saw as a final, irrevocable step.

There was no point in staying in bed any longer. She pushed back the covers and limped across to where her clothes were laid out. For this occasion she would wear her plain travelling dress and cloak and push her heavy hair under a scarf. She had chosen the outfit with care.

The breakfast dishes were laid over chafing dishes to keep toast and scrambled eggs and bacon warm. The smell of them when she lifted the covers made her feel slightly queasy, and she poured herself a cup of tea and drank it quickly.

'Ah, you're awake then!' There was a tap on the door as Mrs O'Byrne put her head round. 'Mrs Grant said you weren't feeling too grand. Not that I'm surprised after all the tossing on the high seas. Sure but God would have fitted us out with fins if He'd meant us to go travelling the oceans! Shall I be warming up the tea?'

'No, thank you. I think I might take a buggy ride. Would it be possible?'

'Charlie comes with his jaunting car around this time. He'll take you where you want to go. I'll catch him for you.' Mrs O'Byrne bustled out again.

Time to write a letter. Rose put down the half-finished tea and rummaged for a sheet of notepaper. She had spent a considerable time working out exactly what she wanted to say. Above all else she wished to guard against leaving Sabre with a bad conscience. It was not his fault that he was unable to love her.

The finished letter gave her a dull satisfaction.

'Dear Aunt Gobnait,

I am afraid this will come as a shock to you but I have been thinking about it for a long time, and if I don't act now I never will. The truth is that I don't love Sabre in the way that a girl ought to love the man she plans to marry. I am very fond of him as a cousin, of course, but marriage needs more than that. Grandmother Fausty used to talk to me often about the early days in Ireland when she was a girl and went to Mass on Sundays, and her sister Mary went to the convent as a nun. It's something I've always wanted to do and never dared tell. Please ask Mother to try to forgive me in time. I know that this will be a terrible disappointment to her, but my mind is made up.

Love,
Rose.'

She had never written so many lies before in her entire life. Later on, when she had become a Catholic, she would have to remember to confess them all.

Sealing the letter and scrawling Gobnait's name across it she was overcome by a sense of futility. Garnet had run away too but she had run towards someone and, no matter what had happened since, there must have been times of happiness for them both. She herself was running away from someone and everything in her cried out against the bleak necessity of it.

'If you're ready for a bit of an airing, Miss, then Charlie's here,' Mrs O'Byrne called up the stairs.

Rose propped the letter on the mantelshelf, pinned her shawl more securely over her head, and picked up her overnight bag. She had a vague feeling that the occasion called for a gesture of some sort but she could think of none to make.

'A bit of air will put the roses back in your cheeks,' Mrs O'Byrne said. Her eyes, missing nothing, flew to the small carpetbag but, the rooms having been paid for in advance, she offered no comment. Even a colleen with a limp had the right to a bit of private life, though from the expression on Rose's face she doubted if she was going to meet a lover.

CHAPTER TEN

Mother Prioress adjusted her veil which was a fraction askew and flicked a speck of dust from her skirt. In her opinion when one took care of the small details the larger ones fell into place. 'Neglect one prayer and the Church begins to totter' was one of the home-grown maxims she regularly trotted out to her novices. Her face, schooled into convent quietness, reflected none of the inner perturbation that assailed her. In her years as a religious she had learned the discipline of detachment but now, faced with her current problem, she felt this virtue eroding.

That Fausty's granddaughter should arrive, demanding admittance to the Order, struck her as coincidence stretched to its limit. Frowning, she dismissed the thought as impious. All things happened according to the Will of God and Rose's arrival might yet be turned to His account.

She closed her eyes briefly, conjuring up after nearly sixty years a picture of her eldest sister, Fausty. She had been dark-eyed and merry, more ambitious than the rest of the family. At seventeen she had gone into England and, though she had sent money and letters through the years, she had never come home again. Mary, safe in the cloister to which

153

she had been dedicated as a child, had heard with deep distaste of the unfortunate affair between her niece, Cathy and her nephew, Patrick. The other children that Fausty had borne seemed equally devoid of moral sense. Gobnait had lived in open adultery with her own sister's husband, Esther had made a runaway match, and Fanny, though nothing to her discredit had come to her aunt's ears, clearly had no notions of propriety, marrying one daughter to Patrick's illegitimate son, permitting another to expose herself on the public stage, and now trying to force the youngest into a marriage with her other cousin! The girl was clearly distressed and equally clearly terrified of her mother. The trouble was that Fausty had apparently abandoned the practice of her religion upon settling in England and from that, the Mother Prioress considered, stemmed all the later scandals. Now this young girl had arrived and in her the older woman saw a brand to be plucked from the burning.

'Mother Prioress, Mrs Grant is still in the parlour.' Sister Angela hovered at the door.

'I will be there in a few moments.' Mother Prioress dismissed her with a nod and frowned as she turned her mental focus upon the visitor.

Gobnait had been Patrick's younger twin, described by Fausty in earlier letters as high-spirited and horse-loving. It was a pity she had

154

not stuck to horses instead of stealing away Fanny's husband and living with him openly. After his death and the death of their daughter she had compounded insult with injury by marrying an old suitor and rushing off to Africa or some such remote place. Now she was back, widowed and running a stud-farm— hardly an occupation for a lady. She must be nearly sixty by now and in her aunt's opinion time had not mitigated her original offences.

She rose, giving her veil a final twitch, and descended the winding stairs to the parlour. Bare and comfortless as a cell, with a barred grille dividing the visitors' section from the enclosure, two chairs faced each other. On one of them, bolt upright with her head flung up as if she imitated one of her beloved horses, a tall, weatherbeaten woman, with plenty of red still visible in her wiry grey hair, stared out of challenging green eyes.

Gobnait was, in fact, so nervous that she was praying silently that her voice wouldn't give out at the last moment. Nothing in her eventful life had prepared her for this cold, bleak building which looked to her more like a prison than anything else. That anyone could voluntarily shut themselves up in such a place was beyond her comprehension. That her pretty niece should have chosen to do so was beyond anybody's comprehension.

'She's run crazy.' Uncle Sean had given his verdict in a flat voice from which everything but shock had vanished.

'Surely to God it's a jape!' Stevie had scratched his head in perplexity. 'She's playing a prank on us.'

'Rose doesn't play pranks,' Gobnait said, 'and you've only to read the letter to know that! She's in deadly earnest.'

'But she's engaged to Sabre. How can she run off into a convent when she's going to be married?' Sean wanted to know.

'It will be Mary's convent. She was asking where it was,' Stevie reminded them.

'Mrs O'Byrne was telling me that she hired a jaunting car and took an overnight bag with her,' Gobnait said.

'That'll be Charlie. I'll have a word with him and find out exactly where he took her,' Sean said, 'but you can take it from me that she's gone to Mary's.'

'So you'd do well to get a good night's sleep before you go chasing after her,' Stevie advised her.

She had wanted to rush to the convent at once, but a moment's reflection convinced her that the advice was sound. They had returned late from the races, flushed with the success of having backed Silver Lady, and by the time they reached the convent it would be after dark. It would do Rose no harm to be granted a night in which to reflect upon her impulsive action, if it had been impulsive. In her letter she said she had been thinking about it for some time. Gobnait had slept fitfully and risen with a headache that throbbed at the back of her neck and was not ameliorated by her cold, echoing surroundings.

'You must be my sister's daughter, Gobnait.'

The voice was cool, with less of an Irish brogue than Gobnait had expected. The woman who seated herself in the chair at the other side of the grille looked, at first sight, so much like Fausty that the other felt a pang, but this woman had the pale complexion of someone who has spent a lifetime immured and her dark eyes were without humour.

'I am Gobnait Grant,' she answered.

'My younger brothers wrote to tell me that you and Fanny's daughter were visiting Ireland, in obedience to a last request of Fausty's.'

'Yes. Yes, Rose gave that as her reason for coming,' Gobnait said. 'Aunt—Mother Prioress, is Rose here? I believe that she took a jaunting car to this convent.'

'I am not aware of her exact mode of transport,' her aunt said.

'Then she is here? I've come to take her home.'

'To be forced into a marriage with her cousin. She has told me about it.'

'Nobody is forcing her into anything,' Gobnait said impatiently. 'This is eighteen seventy-eight, not the Middle Ages!'

'Rose chose here as a refuge from a

marriage that is repugnant to her. I would never turn away a soul in need.'

'She is scarcely a soul in need,' Gobnait argued. 'She coaxed me into coming over to Ireland on the pretext she promised Mother she'd make a pilgrimage here! Two minutes later and she's running off to you with some wild tale of being forced into marriage!'

'Young people frequently express themselves in somewhat exaggerated terms,' the Prioress said tolerantly. 'The fact remains that Rose did come here, seeking sanctuary.'

'Sanctuary from what for Heaven's sake?' Gobnait demanded. 'She and Sabre plan to marry in the spring!'

'She tells me she cannot bring herself to go through with the marriage. She feels very strongly drawn to the life of a religious.'

'Fiddlesticks!' Gobnait's high colour deepened. 'Rose isn't old enough to make such a decision.'

'Yet you consider her old enough to be married.'

'That's different. It's natural to want to be married. I'm sorry. I don't mean to be rude, but I cannot see—and she's not even a Catholic!' Gobnait clutched desperately at a straw. 'Mother didn't bring any of us up in the Faith.'

'I pray that she is not spending much longer in Purgatory on account of it,' the Mother Prioress said drily.

'But she has no notion of what being a nun means,' Gobnait said desperately.

'Nor of what being a Catholic means either. She has not the faintest notion how to use her rosary.'

'That was Mother's. She left it to her.'

'God's Will is worked in surprising ways,' the other said. 'My dear, you must not think me unsympathetic, but there are certain private areas in the life of even a young girl upon which we trespass at our peril. It is possible that the Lord has already marked her down as His own.'

'It's also possible,' Gobnait said sharply, 'that she is suffering from a bad attack of pre-wedding nerves!'

'That too is possible, but I am of the opinion that she may prove to have a genuine vocation,' the Prioress mused.

'The girl's under age and Fanny will never allow it.'

'Sanctuary still means something,' the Prioress said severely. 'Fanny will have to be made to understand that Rose has the right to decide for herself the course of her life. Age has nothing to do with it. Why, I was scarcely fifteen when I entered the novitiate and I knew long before that I would never be happy until I was a bride of Christ.'

'So Rose will be hustled into a habit just because you believed that was the right thing for you to do!'

'My dear, nothing of the kind is going to happen.' For the first time there was warmth in the old woman's voice. 'Rose is welcome to stay here while she searches her own heart. I can arrange for her to receive instruction in the Faith and eventually, if she so wishes, to be received into the Faith. Then, later on, if she displayed, as I believe she will, signs of a true vocation, she could be admitted into the postulancy. Girls spend a year there before they enter the novitiate.'

'I would like to see her.' Gobnait felt as if she had been banging her head against a sponge bag. 'I feel I have the right, at least, to see her.'

'I'll ask her to come down and then she can talk to you alone. I'll bid you goodbye.'

The Prioress rose, sketching on the air a small cross.

'Aunt Mary, this is the first time we ever met,' Gobnait began.

'It may be the last. This is a cloistered Order and we seldom receive visitors.' The other bowed slightly and moved away, opening a door at the side and closing it as she passed through.

Gobnait sat down again, flexing her hands nervously, drawing a deep breath. The interview was over and she had gained nothing. There was an inviolate quality about this place that resisted her.

'Aunt Gobnait.'

160

Rose had entered and stood, hands down at her sides, her head high, at the far side of the grille. In her dark cloak and shawl she looked as if she were already wearing the habit but there were defiant spots of colour in her cheeks and her voice was thin and strained.

'Rose.' Gobnait collected herself and spoke with careful cheerfulness. 'Well, you gave us all quite a fright. What is the trouble, my love?'

'I left a letter.'

'Which made very little sense! What is all this about wanting to be a nun and not wishing to marry Sabre? You cannot be serious.'

'I am completely serious,' Rose said.

'But the marriage is so entirely suitable in every way,' Gobnait said in bewilderment. 'I know Sabre is deeply fond of you.'

'Sabre is a—very nice person,' Rose said with a slight gasp. 'I am deeply attached to him. Indeed I am, but a marriage needs more than that! I am not ready to settle for anything less.'

'But if you don't want to marry Sabre nobody is going to force you,' Gobnait began.

'I don't want to marry anyone,' Rose said. 'I've thought about it for a long time, ever since Grandmother Fausty died, and I'm quite certain. She was a Catholic.'

'Years ago. She hadn't practised for years.'

'But she used to talk about it to me. She made it sound so real, so lovely. The candles and the incense and the chanting.'

'If you've a notion to turn Catholic there's no reason why you shouldn't. I don't imagine Sabre would object.'

'It's more than that,' Rose said. 'I want to study, to—'

'You don't have to be a nun just because you're attracted by Catholicism, and you don't have to marry Sabre if you don't wish,' Gobnait said. She began to feel as if she were hitting her head against the same sponge.

'I want to do what *I* want to do,' Rose said, her voice high and rapid. 'All my life I've done what other people wanted, what Mother always wanted. I'm sorry for deceiving you, for leaving Sabre without telling him, for—I want to stay here. If you make me leave I'll only run away again! You must make Mother understand that.'

'What you need,' said Gobnait in exasperation, 'is a good spanking to bring you to your senses, my girl. This wild idea of yours is the most foolish I ever heard. It will cause a scandal in the family!'

'Then the family should be used to it!' Rose cried, and took a limping step forward, the flush fading from her cheeks. 'I seem to recall nothing but tales of scandal when I came first to England. Uncle Patrick got his Irish cousin into trouble and their bastard married the bastard my mother's first husband fathered on you! And my sister ran off with a travelling actor! Oh, I think that my becoming a Catholic and refusing to marry Sabre is going to be a very small scandal in comparison, don't you?'

'Rose, wait!' Gobnait put out a pleading hand towards the grille, but her niece had turned and was limping rapidly to the door. It opened and shut with a sharp crack that echoed through the parlour.

Dear God, but she had ruined it all! Gobnait sat down again on the hard chair, fury and regret in her face. She had meant to be so calm and reasonable, to use the very real affection there had always been between herself and her youngest niece so that Rose would be persuaded to come home. Instead she had been impatient and Rose had behaved in a way that Gobnait would not have believed possible. She had never heard her gentle niece speak with such bitterness.

The parlour remained empty, the grille a silent barrier between her world and the world into which Rose had fled. The increasing cold made her shiver. If she stayed here any longer she would ache in every joint. In a way she would welcome the pain as a distraction from the sharper pain in her heart. She loved Rose and the prospect of her being wed to Sabre had pleased her immensely. Esther's son and Fanny's daughter were ideally suited, and she had looked forward eagerly to seeing them as husband and wife at Sabre Hall.

The extern Sister who had admitted her was hovering by the door. Gobnait had an urge to

163

rush up to the bars, rattle them vigorously, and scream. If she did that then she would lose any chance of influencing Rose in the future. At least they didn't make girls into nuns overnight and her niece was not even a Catholic yet.

'Thank you, Sister.' She gave the extern nun a brief smile and went down the steps into the courtyard. In the lane the jaunting car was waiting and Sean jumped down as she stepped through the gate.

'What happened? Is she coming back with us then?' he demanded.

'She won't come. She tells me she wants to turn Papist and enter the convent,' Gobnait said and, for one of the few times in her life, burst into humiliating tears.

'Now don't be upsetting yourself, darling girl!' Stevie had joined his brother and was patting her awkwardly on the shoulder. 'Surely it wasn't your fault the silly girl went and lost her mind.'

'Fanny won't look at it that way.' Gobnait groped for a handkerchief and blew her nose vigorously. 'She will blame me for not being an adequate chaperone, and Lord knows what Sabre will say! The poor man is planning to buy the ring as soon as we return home.'

'Perhaps we ought to have gone in with you,' Sean said.

'It wouldn't have done any good. Mary regards us as rascals anyway,' Stevie said. 'She was always a plaster saint even when she was a

164

child! What did Rose have to say? Did she give any explanation?'

'Only that she doesn't want to marry anybody. She wants to stay in the convent.'

'Then she is crazy.' Sean clapped his hat on the back of his head and gave Gobnait a sympathetic look. 'If I were you I'd leave her where she is for the moment. A week of prayers and fasting will likely make her think twice and she'll come bounding back to you, swearing she's made a dreadful mistake!'

'I hope you're right.' Gobnait blew her nose again and climbed up into the cart, thinking gloomily that it was a long time since she had felt so useless.

Rose leaned against the wall beyond the parlour, her eyes closed. She felt limp and drained, with nothing in her but a vast weariness. She had not expected her interview with Gobnait to be an easy one but she had been unprepared for the other's lack of understanding. Her aunt was just like all the others, regarding the marriage as a 'suitable one', and never stopping to think that a girl might wish to be married for reasons other than pity and family convenience.

'Are you feeling quite well, Rose?' The voice of the Mother Prioress penetrated the fog of dull misery in which she was enclosed.

'I am quite well.' She answered with difficulty. 'Aunt Gobnait upset me.'

'There is no need for you to see her again if

you don't wish,' the other said. 'I believe you ought to be given time in which to make up your mind in your own way.'

'And I can stay here? I have a dowry. Nuns require a dowry, don't they?' Rose questioned anxiously.

'All in good time, my dear. You are not even a Catholic yet.'

'But I would like to be. I would like to be a Catholic! Grandmother Fausty was one though she never went to Mass, but she used to talk about it to me sometimes just before she died.'

'Perhaps it was meant for you to make up in some way for her neglect of the Faith,' the older woman said. 'That would be a great and noble mission, wouldn't it?'

'I don't know.' Rose rubbed her fingers across her forehead. 'I can't seem to think straight any longer.'

'Why don't you go into the chapel?' The Mother Prioress indicated an arched doorway. 'I have always found peace and healing there. Later on we can arrange for you to see the Chaplain. He is a very wise and understanding priest, and he will explain everything to you far more clearly than I could and he will give you books to read. Do you like reading?'

'More than anything.' Rose had brightened imperceptibly.

'We have a good library here. You may help Sister Bridget there if you wish to make yourself useful.'

'I do. I don't want to be a burden,' Rose said quickly.

'Go into the chapel now. It's peaceful there.' The Mother Prioress smiled and began to move away.

'If Sabre writes to me,' Rose said, turning back, 'will I have to answer the letter?'

'It would be good manners to answer,' the other said, 'but he may not write.'

'I hope not,' Rose said sadly, and limped away.

Frowning, the Mother Prioress went slowly to her own cell. It was slightly larger than the ones occupied by the rest of the community and contained a flat-topped desk, but was otherwise like them in every respect from narrow bed to wooden crucifix on the wall.

She went first to this, standing with clasped hands, her eyes raised. God, she considered, worked in mysterious ways. Her sister Fausty had neglected and betrayed the Faith, but now a chance for redemption had come in the person of this small, lame girl. If any letters did come then she would make certain Rose would never hear of them. In a life dedicated to God the outside world ought not to be permitted to intrude.

Rose had gone into the chapel and now sat, her eyes fixed on the altar. It was not an elaborate chapel. A series of tiny pictures representing the Stations of the Cross hung around the walls and the altar itself was covered by a plain white cloth on which cross and candlesticks of bronze were neatly set. There were flowers in two vases at each side of the steps and, through the stained-glass window behind, a scatter of sunbeams jewelled the floor. For an instant she was reminded of the gallery at Sabre Hall with its row of stained-glass windows. Then she thrust the memory away. In this place there was no room for regrets.

CHAPTER ELEVEN

'The girl has gone mad,' Fanny said, her voice as tight as her mouth. 'She has clearly gone stark raving mad.'

'You've not heard from her?' Esther enquired.

'No, of course not! I'd have mentioned it if I had. Don't be such a fool, Esther! There was only a letter from Aunt Mary, informing us that she considered the child had a true vocation. A true vocation, if you please! Canting rubbish!'

'She is Mother's sister,' Esther protested weakly.

'She's a Sullivan, and no good ever came from that side of the family. I have written back, telling her that she is to send Rose home at once. I have also made it clear that I am willing to compensate the convent for any expense they may have incurred on her behalf, though she took a hundred pounds out of her allowance with her.'

'I didn't know that,' Gobnait said.

'I would be a very poor kind of mother if I did not make myself aware of such things,' Fanny said coldly. 'I have written also to Rose, telling her that she must remember her duty and come home at once or I will go personally to fetch her.'

'I think that was a mistake,' Gobnait said. 'It will only stiffen her resistance.'

'Rose has no resistance! She's a silly girl of eighteen, nothing more,' Fanny said sharply. 'She will come back and marry Sabre as was arranged.'

'I prefer not.' For the first time Sabre himself joined the conversation. He had been standing, one booted foot on the fender, staring down to the small flames that licked the hearth.

'Sabre, that's foolishness,' Fanny protested. 'I promise you that we will have Rose home within the month. I would go this very moment to fetch her myself, but I fear that with Garnet due any day I simply cannot spare the time! Now you could go, my dear Sabre! There is nothing to prevent you from going to Ireland for a few days.'

'Riding a white horse to storm the convent walls? I didn't know you were that romantic,

Aunt Fanny,' he said wryly.

'I am being practical,' she said impatiently. 'Girls are often nervous before they are married. They get over it when they are faced with the necessity of doing their duty.'

'Surely marriage is more than duty,' Esther said.

'Naturally it is. That goes without saying, but it is also a social obligation. One ought not to make promises that one does not intend to keep! You must travel to Ireland and make her understand that she is to return with you at once.'

'I intend to do no such thing,' he answered.

'Sabre, surely you don't intend to do nothing at all,' Fanny said.

'I am not going to rush off and drag her back by her hair,' he retorted. 'She has the right to change her mind.'

'But she has insulted you,' Fanny said. 'I cannot imagine for one moment that she will continue in her absurd defiance once she sees you face to face.'

'I have written to her,' he said shortly.

'Well, Aunt Mary will surely let her receive letters, won't she?' Esther said hopefully. 'They are not forbidden?'

'I understand she is free to receive letters and to answer them,' Fanny said. 'I hope you made it clear to her that she will quite disgrace the family if she doesn't marry you.'

'The letter was private.' His voice was

gentle, but his eyes, meeting hers, were cold. Her own blue eyes wavered and fell.

'Of course I wouldn't interfere,' she said at last. 'Your marriage is your own affair. However, I would not, even at risk of offending you, neglect my own duty in the matter. Rose is my daughter and, when she behaves badly, that reflects on my training.'

'As when Garnet ran off,' Esther said helpfully and subsided under Fanny's quelling stare.

'Garnet is Lady Ashton now. I am of the opinion that past mistakes should be laid to rest,' she said coldly. 'However, you seem to follow my line of reasoning. Rose's conduct will certainly reflect upon me. To turn down the most suitable alliance in the world in order to hide away in a convent is surely not rational behaviour. The neighbours are bound to talk.'

'That's not very likely,' Gobnait said. 'The engagement was never made public.'

'At Rose's request. Oh, she has been most cunning in this affair. I can only think she takes after you Esther!'

'I'd scarcely call us "cunning",' Esther protested mildly.

'Would you not?' Fanny raised her delicate brows. 'I'm sure I don't know what else you would call it when you, Esther, give birth to a legitimate child and then conspire with Gobnait to conceal the fact until the moment arrives for him to step in and claim his inheritance. One might imagine you feared some danger to him from the rest of the family!'

'Not from the rest of them, no,' Esther said in a low voice.

'If you'll excuse me.' Sabre removed his foot from the fender and stood, impatience in his face, looking at them.

'You're not going out, are you? At a time like this you really ought not to be alone,' Esther began.

'I'm riding over to York,' he said shortly. 'You can discuss family scandal to your heart's content while I'm gone. I am disposed to regard this as a private matter between Rose and myself, though I can appreciate your disappointment.'

'You cannot imagine the extent of it!' Fanny's lip quivered slightly. 'I had set my heart on Rose's becoming mistress of Sabre Hall.'

'No more than I had,' he answered sombrely. 'I may be late, so don't wait up.'

'He will likely get intoxicated and visit a bad woman,' Esther said sadly as the door closed behind him.

'Shame on you, Esther! I didn't think that you knew about such things,' Gobnait said teasingly.

'I am glad you feel able to take it so lightly,' Fanny said. 'My own nature is more sensitive. I blame you for this, you know. You and

Mother! Mother made a pet of Rose, filled her head with rosaries and tales of the good old days and you allowed her to talk you into going to Ireland, where within hours of arriving she'd made her escape.'

'I was her companion, not her gaoler,' Gobnait retorted.

'Unfortunately you were neither,' Fanny said. 'You didn't even bring her away from the convent though you stayed on in Dublin for a full two weeks! I suppose you spent your time in going to race meetings with the uncles.'

'I went back to that damned convent three times,' Gobnait said, beginning to lose her temper. 'Neither Aunt Mary nor Rose would see me! What more could I do?'

'I would have thought of something,' Fanny said grimly. 'As it is we can only hope that Sabre's letter has had some effect. His pride must be quite shattered by her waywardness. I can derive only one crumb of comfort from all this. While Rose is in a nunnery she cannot run off and get involved with anybody else!'

'You always did manage to see the bright side of everything,' Gobnait said drily.

'And the Lord knows that in this family I've had need,' Fanny snapped. 'You are welcome to sneer, but the fact remains I've tried to make the best of a difficult life!'

Sabre had escaped from the confines of the house but not from the questions that hammered at his brain. There was nothing in his life with which to compare what had happened to him. In his thirty-seven years he had been in love on several occasions but the affairs had burned themselves out within a few months, leaving him unscathed. The emotion that had grown up in him for his young cousin had startled him by its intensity. He had never known such tenderness for another human being, nor such an uprush of desire when he thought of his cousin's delicate features and sapphire eyes framed in the unfashionable but oddly-becoming pageboy coiffure of black hair. He had known that she was shy and, for that reason, he had refrained from any expression of passionate affection that might have startled her. He had believed that she was beginning to return his affection, that the love between them would grow and strengthen after they were married. Now it seemed that all his instincts had been mistaken and that, so far was Rose from loving him, that she had fled into a convent rather than go through with the wedding.

He had written to her, stressing his need to see her if only to talk over what was troubling her. He had told her that he would force her to nothing but that he longed to receive a favourable answer. He had tried to write as calmly as he had acted but, when he read his missive through, his emotions, raw and painful, were only too apparent. He had sealed it anyway and gone over to the post office to send it, evading the enquiry of the woman behind the counter who wondered when Miss Rose would be coming home from Ireland.

'And Miss Garnet—Lady Ashton, I ought to say—is coming home, isn't she?' the woman had continued. 'Your Maggie was telling me. To think of Miss Garnet wedding Sir Henry! Well, that will put Miss Victoria's nose out of joint! Always rather uppity was Miss Victoria.'

He had mumbled something and departed, leaving her to remark to her husband, who was nursing a sore tooth by the back fire, that there were others beside Miss Victoria who were uppity if anyone asked her opinion.

Now, saddling his horse, he tried to think of something other than the questions that nagged at him. There was the mill to occupy much of his working day, and the impending visit of Garnet and Sir Henry, and the new stallion to be schooled, and the long nights to be endured. He shook his head at his own foolishness, mounted up and rode out onto the moor. A brisk gallop, followed by a good meal, would clear some of the adolescent cobwebs out of his brain. After that, if he were still in the same restless mood, he would find a woman for the night and pretend, in the darkness, that her flesh was virginal and her eyes blue stars.

He swerved onto the wide track that became a road when it approached the city, and trotted, consciously breathing in the clean, fresh air and noticing the play of colours on the horizon as the sun sank lower. There had been a brief period when he had found the world bright and beautiful without having to remind himself of the fact. Today the breeze made him cough and the colours were muddied.

A coach was approaching, piled high with luggage. He drew rein and pulled his mount aside, raising his hand to greet the driver whom he knew slightly.

'Good-day to you, Mr Ashton!' The man pulled rein too. 'I'm on my way to your place right now. Sir Henry and Lady Ashton are within.'

'Are you Sabre Ashton?' An elderly man with a thatch of grey-white hair put his head out of the coach window and favoured him with a hard stare.

'Yes. You'll be Sir Henry?' Sabre edged his mount nearer, wondering whether to offer to shake hands or not.

'We're on our way to visit you,' Sir Henry said, his severe features relaxing slightly.

'I'll ride back and tell the family that you're here. Welcome, sir.'

'Thank you.' The head was withdrawn, and Sabre had a brief glimpse of a lady in a veiled hat seated at the other side before the coach rolled on again.

So much for a night in York. Good manners demanded that he be present when visitors

176

arrived. Sabre wheeled his horse about and galloped back.

Gobnait was about to make her own departure as he dismounted and he guessed, from the angry flush on her cheekbones, that the argument had continued after he had gone.

'Sir Henry and Garnet are here.' He tossed the reins to Oldfield.

'Today? But we weren't expecting them at once!' Fanny, coming out to the step, looked unaccountably flustered. 'Nothing is ready.'

'Everything is ready, as you know full well,' Gobnait said, 'for there isn't a corner you haven't cleaned almost out of existence!'

'Here they come anyway.' Sabre indicated the laden coach as it lumbered up the hill.

'Esther, do tidy yourself up.' Fanny went to the door to call within, and turned back again, the anxiety in her eyes masked by an expression of excited pleasure as the coach gained the flat sweep of grass and the driver clambered down to open the door.

Sir Henry looked younger and more sprightly than the last time they had met. Then he had been testy with gout and fretful about Victoria. Now he looked as if a new lease of life had been granted him.

'Fanny, my dear.' He came forward, leaning only slightly on his stick. 'It has been a long time but it's good to be here.'

'You are most welcome!' She took his hand

177

in her own, her blue eyes moving past him to where Garnet stood, tall in elegant grey silk, her features blurred by the veil. Then she dropped Sir Henry's hand and went forward, reaching up to embrace her daughter.

'My dear, I am so very glad to have you with us again,' she said warmly. 'I am so pleased about your marriage. Henry is a fine man and you are a most fortunate young lady. But here we are, all standing in the wind when you must be worn out. Come inside at once! Sabre, have you introduced yourself properly yet? Henry, this is Esther's son.'

'And Philip's,' Sir Henry said. He took a step forward and bowed somewhat stiffly. In his expression was the memory of that long-ago marriage when his brother had eloped with Esther Sabre and the course of his own life had changed in consequence. Then he smiled faintly, as if dismissing the past, and shook hands with the younger man as they went into the hall.

'I'll have Maggie bring some tea. Esther, see to it, will you?' Fanny was leading the way into the dining room. 'Gobnait, you'll stay for a cup of tea, won't you? Garnet, do take off your hat and let us all see you properly. This passion for veiling is quite beyond me. In my young days it was tiny off-the-face bonnets.'

Garnet was unpinning her hat and smoothing back her heavy knot of brown hair. Revealed, her face was Gobnait's, cast in a much younger, sterner mould, the long eyes grey instead of green. Sabre, shaking hands, thought he had never felt such a limp clasp nor seen such indifference in a girl's face.

'I'm glad to meet you,' he said, more cordially than he felt, the cancelled evening in York still irritating him.

'And I you.' She had a low, husky voice that would have been attractive had it not been so toneless. 'Where is Rose?'

She had asked the question of Fanny and there was an instant's embarrassed silence before the latter answered smoothly.

'Rose is still in Ireland. She and Gobnait went there on a visit and Rose was so taken with the country that she is staying on for a while.'

'I thought that she and cousin Sabre—' The grey eyes moved to him.

'Oh, Rose is still very young. It will be spring at least before anything can be arranged,' Fanny said, smiling. 'You know, Mother's last wish was that Rose should make a sentimental pilgrimage to Dublin. She's staying with the uncles, Sean and Stephen, but she may spend a few weeks with my Aunt Mary. She's a nun, but I'm told they have guest rooms in the convent. Ah! here's the tea! Maggie, you had better start supper. We had planned quite a feast, Henry, but you have taken all of us rather by surprise.'

'My affairs were wound up sooner than I

expected,' Sir Henry said. 'We decided to travel north.'

'I've given you Pearl and Larch's old rooms,' Fanny said.

For the first time there was a slight ripple of feeling across Garnet's smooth, blank countenance.

'It seems so odd,' she said, 'not to see Pearl and Larch or Grandmother Fausty here, and now Rose has gone too.'

'And Sabre is come.' Fanny smiled at her nephew. 'It's all comings and goings these last few years, I can tell you.'

'The news of Sabre's existence was certainly a surprise,' Sir Henry said, with a slight return of his former coldness.

'Oh, Esther was always a dark horse,' Fanny said. 'Henry, do tell me how Victoria is! I hope she will be coming to visit us soon. Now that you and Garnet are married I think it time that this entire family feud be buried.'

'Victoria is still in London. She is seeing to the sale of my town house and will probably come up later,' Sir Henry said.

'Victoria has been very kind,' Garnet said expressionlessly.

'Then you mean to settle here, sir?' Sabre said. The 'sir' was too formal, but he couldn't think of the man as his uncle.

'Garnet is happier in Yorkshire and, provided we spend part of the winter in a warmer clime, I shall be happy to return to my

180

roots too,' he answered. 'Ashton House was sold and is, in any event, too large for us. I shall use my time here to look out for a smaller property.'

'Will Victoria live with you?' Esther asked.

'I think she will certainly spend some time here,' Sir Henry said, 'but she's a very independent young lady and has her own circle of friends.'

'Well, we shall be delighted to see her,' Fanny said warmly.

She glanced towards Sabre with the evident expectation of having her invitation seconded, but he was staring at Garnet. He had never beheld a woman with such a completely fixed and immobile face. Even her eyes were devoid of life. It was difficult to reconcile the stiff figure who answered in such a mechanical fashion with the description that Rose had given him of the lively sister who had defied convention and run away with an actor.

'I'd better be going.' Gobnait put down her teacup and stood up. 'I'm happy to see you, Garnet. You too, Henry, and I wish you both joy. Will you ride over to see me as soon as you're fully recovered from your journey?'

'Garnet is not riding at present,' Sir Henry said. 'In her condition—and the physician is fairly certain—horseback riding is really not very wise.'

There was a moment's silence, in the midst of which Sabre was surprised to feel within

181

himself a violent repugnance to the notion of his cousin's being pregnant by a husband old enough to be her grandfather.

'My dear, I couldn't be more delighted!' A beaming Fanny embraced her daughter who received the caress with an indifference that bordered on hostility.

'Good Lord! What a tangle it will be,' Esther said, 'trying to explain the relationships within the family to the poor child! Why Garnet is not only Sabre's cousin but his aunt by marriage, and Henry is my nephew by marriage as well as my brother-in-law!'

'Come and see me anyway,' Gobnait said. 'Come in the pony trap, for that can't do you any harm.'

'I'll come in a day or two,' Garnet said, extricating herself from her mother's arms. 'You look very well, Aunt.'

'I'm well preserved, like an old relic,' Gobnait said. 'See me out, Sabre, will you?'

He went thankfully, glad to shake off the cross-currents of tension in the room.

As he helped his aunt to mount, he couldn't avoid saying,

'How does Garnet seem to you? This is the first time we've met.'

'She's not the girl I remember,' she answered briefly. 'God knows what happened between her and that actor, or why she agreed to marry Henry, but sooner or later she may confide in me. To be with child already! She's scarcely two months wed.'

'He seems a pleasant enough man,' Sabre observed.

'Oh, Henry was always a dry stick,' Gobnait said, gathering up the reins in her long, capable hands. 'Wanted to be a clergyman when he was young. I sometimes think that he'd have been a happier man if he'd never become Sir Henry! Well, he seems contented enough with Garnet.'

'And she?' He frowned the question.

'Garnet is not the girl I remember,' she repeated. 'She will talk to me in her own good time. Sabre, is there anything else you want me to do about Rose? I could write or go back to Ireland, but my own instinct is to let matters lie for a while. She will come to her senses more quickly if she's not pushed and pulled in all directions at once.'

'I've written to her and let her know how deeply I care about her,' he said.

'Do you, Sabre?' Her green eyes were soft as she looked at him. 'You know Rose is fortunate to have someone love her like that. I knew such a love, long ago when Matthew Lawley was alive. We defied the world and lived together for years—the happiest years I ever knew. There's no bar to a marriage between you and Rose, save her own feelings in the matter, and it would be a very great tragedy if all didn't go well.'

'I'll not force her.'

'Of course not.' She leaned forward, patting his lean cheek in a rare gesture of affection, then, as if ashamed of her momentary lapse into sentiment, hit her mount with the flat of her hand and sent it bounding forward.

He watched her out of sight, then went back, not through the front door, but round to the side where the scent of baking drifted through the kitchen into the cobbled yard. He could see Maggie bustling about within and then the door was pushed wider and Garnet stepped out, holding her skirt clear of the cobbles.

'I came to see the horses,' she said by way of explanation. 'They were always my best friends here.'

'Aunt Gobnait said you liked to ride,' he remembered.

'I used to ride with Cousin Larch. He was married to my sister, but Pearl never cared for horses. You never met them, of course.'

'Their deaths must have been a great shock,' he said sympathetically.

'At the time.' She wandered past him into the stables and began a slow perambulation past the stalls, pausing now and then to greet an old friend. Without looking at him she said, 'One gets over things more quickly than one expects.'

'So they say.' He followed her, leaning against the open door, watching her tall, slim shape moving about in the gloom.

'Why did Rose stay in Ireland?' She had turned and was watching him. He sensed sharpness in her eyes.

'You heard what Aunt Fanny said,' he countered.

'You think that I believe what my mother tells me?' She gave a tinkling, artificial laugh that grated on him. 'Why is Rose not here? You and she are engaged, aren't you?'

'She wanted time to think,' he said uncomfortably. 'I fear she has the idea that she's being thrust into this without having any choice in the matter.'

'We none of us have any choice in the end,' Garnet said in a harsh voice. 'If Rose would learn that she would be a happier person.'

'Are you happy?' he asked bluntly.

'Of course I am.' She came towards him, a little smile on her mouth, her eyes blank as if no thoughts moved behind them. 'My husband is rich and amiable and it's more than likely that I am carrying his child. I am very happy.'

They had only just been introduced and it was unforgivable of him, but he said it anyway.

'What of your lover? What happened to him?'

'Nicholas?' Her composure didn't waver for an instant. 'That unfortunate misalliance is over and done. He was married to someone else all the time and that gave me the chance to leave and do what I really wished to do.'

'To marry Sir Henry Ashton?'

'Exactly so!' She gave him a brisk nod and walked past him, still smiling. 'If you will excuse me, cousin, I must see to the unpacking. It is most kind of you to entertain us here. It cannot be easy to have complete strangers thrust upon one, but I promise you that we'll be moving into permanent accommodation very soon.'

'I sometimes feel that I am a stranger here,' he said.

'Your existence certainly came as a surprise,' she agreed, and gave the light, hard laugh again, as she went into the kitchen.

Frowning after her, Sabre wondered if his cousin's arrival would cause the trouble he could sense beginning, or if it would come out in some other way.

CHAPTER TWELVE

'My dear, this must be a happy day for you!'

The Mother Prioress spoke with unusual warmth, her eyes on the small grey-clad figure who stood before her.

'Yes, Reverend Mother.' Rose answered brightly, mindful of the rule that postulants were supposed always to be cheerful.

'A sullen, miserable postulant gives no glory to God and reflects no credit upon her Community,' the Novice Mistress was fond of saying.

'To be received into the Holy Faith and into the Postulancy on the same day, after only six months, is quite an achievement. You must give thanks to God for the graces with which He has showered you,' the Prioress continued.

'Yes, Reverend Mother.' Rose hesitated, then ventured, 'I wonder if—if there was any word from home—from Sabre Hall, I mean.'

'My dear child, don't you think I would have given you any letters that came?' the other reproached.

'I beg your pardon, Reverend Mother.' Rose's cheeks had flushed slightly.

'As this is a special day we will waive the penance,' the Prioress said.

'Thank you Reverend Mother.' The flush faded.

'So!' The older woman leaned back, folding her hands within the wide sleeves of her habit. 'For this next year you will be in the Postulancy. At the end of that time, if you so wish and if you are deemed suitable by the Community, you will enter the Novitiate for a period of two years when your training proper will begin.'

'Yes, Reverend Mother.'

'Because you are my great-niece,' the Prioress said, 'I must confess that I take an especial interest in your progress, though I strive not to show favouritism. However, I am of the opinion that God sent you to us for a reason. My sister, Fausty, God rest her soul, entirely neglected the tenets of her Faith after she went to England and, for that reason, failed to give her children the firm guidance they needed. You know the unhappy history of your family, the scandals, the misalliances. I believe that in you is the chance to make reparation. I urge nothing at all because you are free to choose. Our doors are locked on the inside, not the outside. But if you choose the path of sacrifice, the way of renunciation, then who can measure the spiritual riches you will amass for yourself and those whom you love.'

'I shall try, Reverend Mother.' Rose spoke earnestly, her blue eyes shining.

'Go into the chapel now and ask the Lord to guide your decision. You are excused duties for the rest of the day. Yes, what is it?'

Rose, hesitating at the door, said tentatively, 'I wonder if I ought to write to them at—at Sabre Hall, to tell them that I am a postulant.'

'Do you wish to write?'

'It would—yes, I would like to explain. They might write back to me.'

'If you wish to write personally then you are naturally free to do so,' the Prioress said slowly. 'On the other hand, what a glorious start to your religious life if you were to deny yourself that small, personal indulgence. It would be a foundation stone in the wall of detachment that every nun must build. I could write on your behalf, if you like.'

'Would you, Reverend Mother? I'd not want them to think I'd forgotten them or stopped loving them,' Rose said.

'I think you may depend on me to use the right words,' the Prioress said.

'Thank you, Reverend Mother.' Rose curtsied and went out, closing the door noiselessly as the rules demanded.

The chapel had become her refuge. She made her way to her usual place and sank to her knees, crossing herself with the care of a convert. Ahead of her the great window glowed, catching and transmuting the spring sunshine into jewels of light. The winter had been cold and damp but summer lay ahead. At Sabre Hall the daffodils would be springing up and Sabre would be exercising the colts. She winced, having broken her own private rule never again to think of her cousin. If he had only written to her, just once, to ask her to reconsider her decision! He had made no protest, sent no word of argument. That proved that her decision had been the right one. He had been willing to marry her out of a sense of family obligation, but his feelings for her had not been strong enough for him to protest against the breaking of their engagement. The hope that had lain for months in the bottom of her heart flickered and died in the light from the stained-glass window.

The Prioress, moving back her chair, pulled open the drawer in the desk and frowned at the bundle of letters within. Several, couched in vituperative terms, were from Fanny. Really, her niece seemed to be a most unpleasant woman! There were also three letters from Sabre Ashton, two of them couched in sensible, affectionate terms, the third containing what even the Prioress recognised as a declaration of love. Her lips thinned slightly. Rose was so young and so pure. It was a kindness to save her from the lusts of the flesh. After a moment she closed the drawer again and reached for pen and paper. She would write to Fanny, telling her of Rose's conversion and her reception into the Postulancy, making it clear that the child was doing everything out of her own free will.

*   *   *

Sabre had a headache, the result of a too convivial evening spent at York. He had been half-inclined to stay on for a day or two and get the restlessness out of his system, but waking in a rumpled bed beside a woman whose name he hadn't even troubled to enquire had induced in him such a spasm of disgust that he had flung on his clothes and ridden back, the pounding of his horse's hooves echoing the pounding in his skull.

He had left the main track almost without

realising it, swerving over the hill to the white-painted farmhouse with its attendant stables and barn. Gobnait, in breeches and jersey, was mucking out as he rode up, and he couldn't repress a smile as she leaned the rake against the wall and strode to greet him, apparently oblivious to the dirt on her face.

'Been out carousing?' She gave him a shrewd, fleeting glance. 'Do you need a hair of the dog or a black coffee?'

'Neither. I'm on my way down to the mill as soon as I've changed my clothes.' He looked down at her, feeling as he always did a warm comradeship with her. He was fond of his mother, though the knowledge she had virtually abandoned him when he was small set a bar to deeper intimacy, and he respected his Aunt Fanny, but in Gobnait he sensed a wide-reaching tolerance and a love of life that triumphed over all odds.

Impulsively he said, 'Tell me how you bore it when you lost someone you loved.'

'I don't know.' She pushed back a strand of greying hair, answering him slowly. 'I thought I would never recover from Matthew's death, but I had Abigail then to care about and the horses. Matthew worked hard to build up the stud-farm and I couldn't let all his work go for nothing. I worked, I suppose. And then Edward Grant came into my life again. He'd always wanted to marry me. We used to joke about it. But Edward came back and he didn't mind about my having been another man's mistress. He still wanted me for his wife, and he was a good husband. We travelled together, explored, laughed, were good friends. It wasn't as it had been with Matthew but there was a sweetness in it all the same. You will find someone else, Sabre. You're rich and handsome, a catch for any girl. There'll be one along.'

'And it won't matter who she is,' he said, moodiness darkening his face. 'She won't be Rose.'

'There's no word?'

'Not since the Prioress wrote to Aunt Fanny. Rose has turned Catholic and become a postulant. Finish.'

'But she's not taken nun's vows yet. Sabre, why don't you go to Ireland? Take a train to Liverpool and catch the ferry from there. Insist on an interview with her. At least you'll be able to see her face to face! Fanny can manage the mill and I'll take responsibility for the horses while you're away. Why don't you?' she urged.

'Because I'll not force her into doing what she has no wish to do,' he answered. 'Aunt, I'm not a completely insensitive fool. I'm fond of Aunt Fanny but I can see the way she tries to dominate everybody who comes near her. Garnet ran away, didn't she? Rose was willing to marry me to please her mother but, in the end, she couldn't face it and she ran away too. I won't bully her into doing what isn't in her heart to do.'

'Then I hope someone comes along soon,' Gobnait declared, 'before you ruin your health with more overnight jaunts in York. If you won't have any refreshment you'll excuse me if I get on! The new lad's taken the day off to go to a funeral. As it's the third time he's made that excuse in the last couple of months I can only assume either that he's the most shocking little liar or that he comes from a singularly unfortunate family!'

'I'll see you, Aunt!' Grinning, despite the pain in his head and the misery that coursed through him, he raised his hand in farewell and cantered down the slope.

*   *   *

'If I grow any fatter,' Garnet declared, 'I will have to remember what my feet look like, for it's certain I'll not be able to see them!'

'Does your back still ache, dear?' Esther looked up sympathetically from the flowers she was arranging. 'I can make some more rosemary tea for you.'

'Thank you but no. I'm so full of tea that I shall soon begin to float.'

'Only a little time to go. The last days are always the worst,' Esther said, pushing a recalcitrant daffodil into place and giving it a warning glance. 'I can recall how perfectly dreadful I felt before Sabre was born.'

'It must have been worse for you,' Garnet said.

'You mean because Philip had died and I was in a foreign country? Yes, it was hard, but I had to take care of myself for the baby's sake.'

'Yet you left him, to be reared by strangers.'

'I was afraid the Ashtons might claim him,' Esther said vaguely, 'and later on—it seemed best to leave him where he was. I used to wonder sometimes if he had grown up to look like Philip. He has in a way, but he has Sabre eyes. Like my father. That was a great consolation to me.'

'That he had eyes like your father?' Garnet asked in faint surprise.

'That I had borne a child to the man I loved,' Esther said. 'You will find that a great blessing in the future.'

'Henry is not yet dead,' Garnet said coldly.

'No, dear.' Esther glanced at her. 'I was not thinking of Henry at that moment. Now have you thought of names?'

'I thought Philip,' Garnet said. 'That's if you don't object?'

'Not in the least. Philip is a good name and holds very sweet associations for me. Certainly not Henry,' Esther said, reverting to her normal vagueness. 'Not Nicholas either. That would never do—and here is Fanny! We were just wondering where you were, dear.'

'I've been helping Henry to draw up a list of

suitable properties in the district,' Fanny said. 'He is seriously considering having a new house built.'

'That would take a couple of years,' Garnet said.

'Well, there's no hurry for you to move,' Fanny observed. 'Sabre has been most generous about giving up his rooms to you and is very nicely settled in Mother's old room, and moving house is not the way in which to launch a new baby into life. A small child requires a settled environment for the first year or two. You will call him Earl, I suppose?'

'Philip,' Garnet informed her.

'Philip? Oh, I think not, dear. That name would arouse too many memories,' Fanny said kindly. 'Henry would be constantly reminded of the breach with his own brother. Earl would be an ideal choice, the two names symbolising the union of our two families after so many years of disagreement and suspicion.'

'Earl then, if you wish.'

'It will be a funny name for a girl,' Esther remarked.

'If it's a girl we shall call her Faustina, of course. Do not try to be foolish, Esther,' Fanny said patiently. 'Garnet, you cannot possibly be doing yourself any good by slumping in that manner. You ought to take some gentle exercise.'

'I'll go down and take a stroll in the garden,' Garnet said, heaving herself to her feet.

'Put your shawl on. The wind's quite keen. I shall go down later on and sweep the paths. Maggie never finds time to do them properly.'

'I'll tell her on the way out,' Garnet said.

'She takes very little interest in anything these days,' Fanny remarked, staring after her. 'I hope she perks up when the child is actually born. Infants are sensitive to moods.'

'It's hard, having the first baby,' Esther said.

'As you only bore one child in your entire life,' Fanny said, 'I fail to see how you can make the comparison. In fact Rose caused me the worst trouble. That was a most difficult birth!'

'I wish Rose were not in the convent,' Esther said, abandoning her flower arrangement and sitting down again.

'You cannot wish it more than I do,' Fanny said. 'A marriage between her and Sabre would have been ideal, made in Heaven! As owner of Sabre Hall he really ought to marry!'

'We shall have to wait and see what happens,' Esther said.

'If Garnet had—but Henry does seem very much improved in health since he came back to Yorkshire.' Fanny paused, drumming her fingers on the sill.

In the garden below Garnet paced slowly down the path, her shawl wrapped round her swollen figure. She was not unhappy. She had reached a stage when she no longer felt any emotion at all. There was nothing in her body but the burden of her kicking child, nothing in her head but the thought that when it was over she would be free to ride again, and there was nothing in her heart at all.

'My dear, I saw you from the window!' Sir Henry hurried out to join her. 'You ought to rest more at this stage, you know. I recall that, before Victoria was born, Elizabeth used to lie down every afternoon.'

'Elizabeth was delicate. I'm exceedingly healthy,' Garnet said.

'Even so.' He gave her a fretful look, wondering why she seemed so remote, more remote than before he had married her. At the back of his mind was the disappointment of having married a frigid woman when he had courted a sensual one.

'I have been thinking we might build a house instead of buying an existing one though I shall naturally continue to look at local properties,' he said. 'I really feel we ought not to trespass on your mother's hospitality any longer.'

'The house belongs to Sabre,' Garnet said shortly.

'One forgets.' Sir Henry frowned. 'I still find it difficult to accept the fact that he is my brother's son. If proof were required of Esther's weakness of intellect it would surely be found in her long concealment of his existence. Fanny was right.'

'Right?' Garnet enquired.

'She knew that marriage would be too much for Esther. When she learned that there was an attachment between Philip and Esther she had the courage to go privately to my mother and inform her of Esther's condition. Unhappily Philip defied everybody and eloped with her.'

'So that was it.' Garnet spoke with an intake of breath.

'Esther is ignorant of the circumstances surrounding the original quarrel between our families,' Sir Henry said. 'To tell you the truth I find myself quite fond of her, though her vague manner is intensely irritating. Your mother is a saint to be so patient with her.'

'Saint Fanny,' Garnet said and drew in her breath again.

'Is anything wrong?' He looked at her in concern. 'You look quite pale!'

'I have a cramp.' She bent over suddenly, retching.

'The child is not due for nearly a month!' Sir Henry looked round wildly, his usual poise deserting him.

'Babes sometimes arrive early, fool!' Garnet had reached the bench and was clinging to it, sweat beading her forehead.

'Stay there! I'll get Fanny.' He hurried back, raising his voice to call out.

'But I don't want Mother,' Garnet thought in anguished confusion. 'I want Nicholas. He won't come. He won't ever come again, but that doesn't stop me from wanting him.'

It was a cruel irony that she should again begin to long for him at the moment when she was at her most unattractive. Then she forgot irony and longing in the humiliation of breaking waters and jumbled sounds of voices calling across the garden.

*   *   *

'Earl Sabre!' Fanny took another look at the swaddled bundle.

'Earl Ashton, my dear Fanny,' Sir Henry corrected. 'His surname is Ashton.'

'I meant that he is going to be the image of his great-grandfather. Dark auburn hair and his eyes—possibly a darker grey? What do you think, Gobnait?'

'That you're making a positive fool of yourself over that baby,' Gobnait said tolerantly.

'My first grandchild.' Fanny accepted the rebuke with smiling good-humour. 'I shall likely indulge him grossly, but a little spoiling never hurt a child.'

'I never heard you say that before,' Gobnait remarked.

'Well, someone has to spoil him,' Fanny argued. 'Garnet won't take the slightest interest in him at all. She could feed him herself with a little effort but she refuses even to try!'

'Garnet had a very bad confinement. She must be feeling very weak.'

'The word I would have employed is indifferent,' Fanny contradicted. 'I shall have to employ a good wet-nurse. Annie Watkins is here now, but there's a history of consumption in her family and I'll be much happier to find a more robust nurse. If it were left to Garnet, that poor babe would starve to death. Premature babes require very careful handling!'

'He was a good weight for an eight-month child,' Gobnait commented.

'Six pounds. Had he been a full term he might have proved too large for her to deliver without real danger,' Fanny said.

'Henry is pleased anyway.'

'It has taken ten years off his age,' Fanny smiled. 'Do you know the first thing he did was to journey to York to see his lawyer there? He told me privately that, at his death, Garnet will have one-third of his entire estate and Earl will receive two-thirds of what remains. He will be an exceedingly rich little boy one day.'

'Henry seems healthy enough,' Gobnait said. 'Ten years off his age you said?'

'Metaphorically speaking—not that I wish Henry any harm. He's a very dear old friend and my son-in-law!'

'A son-in-law older than yourself,' Gobnait murmured.

'Not so much older, and age matters so little

when it's a question of affairs of the heart.'

'Will you write to the convent?'

'Rose has broken her word and disappointed me deeply, but she is still my daughter,' Fanny said. 'I shall write and inform her that Garnet has borne a son. Oh, the girl was disobedient once, but she has made up for it since. I am pleased with Garnet.'

'Poor Rose.' Gobnait sighed.

'Rose has made her own bed and is doubtless lying on it,' Fanny said repressively. 'Henry wishes you and Sabre to be godparents, by the bye.'

'I shall go to York and buy him a pony,' Gobnait said.

'He is rather small to start any equestrian pursuits,' Fanny said.

'They can grow up together. I shall give him his first lesson.'

'Unless Sabre wishes to do so,' Fanny said.

'By then I hope Sabre will have found another woman and be on the way to siring an heir of his own,' Gobnait retorted.

'I think it more likely that Sabre will remain faithful to the affection he bears Rose,' Fanny said. 'He was most deeply enamoured of her.'

'I'm surprised you don't rush off to Ireland and drag her back by force,' the other remarked.

'I have never forced anyone to do anything against their will,' Fanny said coldly. 'Rose has chosen her path and Sabre—well, it would be most insensitive of me to try to thrust him into a loveless marriage!'

'And if Sabre never marries,' Gobnait said slowly, 'then the property eventually passes to Garnet's boy.'

'I hadn't thought of that.' Fanny bent over the cradle again, her blue eyes fond. 'Earl may be very rich indeed one day.'

'A long way off. Sabre is extremely healthy.'

'Of course.' Fanny bent lower, stroking her grandson's apple smooth cheek.

*   *   *

'So I know you will join with me in wishing joy and long life to your half-brother. Earl is a handsome child and good-tempered since a more suitable wet-nurse was found. Garnet has regained much of her physical strength but continues somewhat listless.'

Victoria let her father's letter flutter to the dressing table. She had read it several times and the news it contained did not grow any more palatable with repetition. In the mirror her face looked strained and pale, the elaborately curled fair hair a frame for discontent.

The marriage of her father to Garnet Webber had struck her as an obscenity, not only because of the difference in their ages but because Garnet was a member of the family from which Victoria had been guarded all her life.

'The Sabres are not our kind. We have nothing to do with them,' had been a precept drummed into her since childhood.

She had known Larch, the handsome boy born of the affair between Patrick Sabre and his Irish cousin. There had been a time when she and Larch had been very close indeed, but nothing had come of it and, her father having decided to leave Yorkshire, she had locked up her dreams and gone dutifully with him. She had not even wept when the word of Larch's death had come.

And then, with no warning, her father had married Garnet despite all Victoria's previous attempts to forestall it. Why she had not married her lover was a question Victoria would dearly have liked to have answered, but she knew it would be impossible ever to ask.

And now this! A half-brother, to dispossess her of much that was rightfully hers. A proof that her respectable, elderly father went to bed and did unspeakable things with his hussy of a wife. Worse than that was the nagging possibility that, unless Sabre married, that property too would one day pass to Earl.

Victoria, contemplating the future, came to a swift, irrevocable decision. At thirty-seven she was still attractive, still of an age to be married and bear children, and Sabre Ashton had no wife.

Rose was polishing the wooden altar rail, the scent of beeswax drifting up from the dark wood. She rubbed energetically, her attention fiercely concentrated on the task in hand. Garnet and Sir Henry had a son, a little baby, named Earl after her grandfather. Her mother had written to the Prioress, adding that it was time Rose came to her senses and went home, but from Sabre there had been no word.

In Rose's blue eyes tears were gathering and glistening, falling on the polishing cloth. She drew a quivering breath, repeating silently one of Grandmother Fausty's favourite maxims.

'When things look bad,' Fausty had been fond of saying, her dark eyes merry, 'wait a little because they always look better when morning comes.'

But in this place, for her, Rose thought, morning would never come again.